A Hustler's Promise 2: Promise Kept

Jackie Chanel

Published by Bold As Love Media

Copyright 2011 Jackie Chanel

Cover Art by April Harris, Bold As Love Media

ISBN: 1475121407
ISBN-13: 978-1475121407

Praise for A Hustler's Promise: Some Promises Won't be Broken

This was a highly entertaining and quick read. It flowed very well and kept my attention. I highly recommend this book! - Cheryl, Black Diamond Book Reviews

A Hustler's Promise has all the elements of contemporary fiction and urban romance. - Crystalsteeler (Amazon Review)

Love, action, and intrigue--this book has it! - A.K Taylor, author of *Neiko's Five Land Adventure*

Get Part I Today! You don't want to miss the beginning!

"I believe that everything that you do bad comes back to you. So everything that I do that's bad, I'm going to suffer from it. But in my mind, I believe what I'm doing is right. So I feel like I'm going to heaven."
Tupac Amaru Shakur

CHAPTER 1

Jaicyn Jones stared out the bay window in the master bedroom of her dream house and sighed.

Despite the low temperature, the sun was shining brightly through the clouds. Even after spending three winters in Atlanta, she still hadn't gotten used to the sky being so bright in the winter. Winters in Washington Heights were always cold and dreary.

She ran her hand along the window sill and touched the designer pillows that were only to be used as window decorations. There were many "look but don't touch" decorations in her house. She'd gone a little overboard but at the time, she didn't care. She was decorating her house the way she wanted to, with her boyfriend's approval of course.

My house, she thought to herself and smiled.

Gone was the rundown townhouse in Washington Heights. She never had to go back there again. She wasn't fifteen and trying to survive the cold hard streets of anymore. No more tiny apartment in the West End of Atlanta either. She had her very own house in a suburban community in Stone Mountain! Rayshawn had come through for her once again.

"Jaicyn!" she heard her boyfriend, Rayshawn, call her name from downstairs. His impatient tone made her lose her focus. She tightened the sash on her Coach trench coat and walked out of the master suite.

"I said I was coming!" she yelled back. "It's my birthday! Stop rushing me!"

"I don't care," Rayshawn said as she tip-toed down the stairs in a pair of red bottoms with four and a half-inch heels.

"Jay-Jay," Rayshawn groaned. "We're on our way to the storage unit, not some damn fashion show. Go change."

"Relax babe, I have sneakers in my bag."

No matter what her man said, Jaicyn wasn't changing. She'd spent hours in the salon getting her hair cut, styled, and highlighted and even more hours in Lenox Mall picking out the perfect pair of Louboutins and her birthday outfit. Her birthday only came once a year.

"Go get in the car," Rayshawn grumbled.

Jaicyn wondered why he was so uptight. They'd made the trip to the storage unit plenty of times. There was nothing exceedingly special about today. Same shipment, same driver, same routine. Yet, her man was more tense over a drop off than she'd ever seen him.

When she, her two sisters, and Rayshawn moved to Atlanta three years ago, Jaicyn had no idea that life could be so good in the South. Atlanta was the perfect place for her and Rayshawn to set up shop and make a ton of money for themselves and the leader of Washington Height's notorious drug crew, Andre "King" Carter.

At least in theory.

Washington Heights was a rough place but it was nothing compared to a city the size of Atlanta, Georgia. Rayshawn had spent six months in

Atlanta helping King set up his piece of the drug empire. When they came back to Washington Heights everything in the "A" was fine.

Neither Jaicyn nor Rayshawn suspected that the real reason that Little Man wanted to come home had nothing to do with his baby-mama or his kids. The Atlanta dealers wanted him out. He had no choice but to haul ass back to Washington Heights.

Little Man was soft. Rayshawn and Jaicyn were sent to Atlanta because they could do everything that Little Man wasn't cut out to do. If they didn't know how to do anything else, they knew how to sell drugs and make money. They ran the tightest crew in Washington Heights. The Atlanta dealers wouldn't have a clue what hit them when the Prince and Princess rolled through the town and took over.

At least that was Jaicyn's thought when King proposed them moving to Atlanta.

As she fidgeted in the driver's seat of her brand new Dodge Charger, Jaicyn thought back to the first rough months in Atlanta. The memories of shootouts and fights sent a shiver through her body. She clutched her Coach bag and felt the cool steel of her nine millimeter Glock. The coolness eased the memory. Her Glock had been her best friend when Rayshawn put her in charge of two of the four crews he and King had assembled.

No man likes to take orders from a woman, especially not a brassy and tough chick like Jaicyn. They had their girlfriends, sisters, and baby-mamas ambush her on the streets, in clubs, even once in the parking lot of Costco. With no one to help her and Rayshawn across town handling his own set of problems, Jaicyn had no choice but to fight and Jaicyn Jones had long stopped fighting fair after being shot at in Washington Heights.

When Rayshawn got word that Jaicyn's life was in danger – of course *she* wasn't the one who told him – he wanted to yank her off the streets and keep her hot tempered ass in the house. Atlanta chicks weren't afraid of her like the girls were back home. Neither were the guys.

Jaicyn's reputation for being a "take no shit" kind of boss in Washington Heights hadn't followed her down south. No one knew she had held a girl at gunpoint and pressed her for information. The dealers in Atlanta didn't care that she was the mastermind behind the sneak attack that had left two drug dealers floating in Lake Erie.

She and Rayshawn were the new kids on the block, no matter *who* had sent them. They had to earn the respect that they thought they deserved. Little Man wasn't prepared for it. He thought King's reputation would be enough. Jaicyn was the only one who knew that she'd have to show the city of Atlanta who was boss, just like she had in Washington Heights. So she fought, with her fists when necessary, and with her gun when her lethal right hook wasn't enough.

Rayshawn tapped on her window interrupting her thoughts. "What's wrong?"

Jaicyn shook her head. "Nothing. I just want to get this over with. I don't want to spend my birthday making drop offs."

"Don't snap at me," Rayshawn grunted. "I told him not to come until tomorrow." He got into his own car and the engine purred to life.

Jaicyn leaned forward and turned up the new Jay-Z CD that was playing and took her Blackberry out of her purse and immediately began texting her crew. If she had to spend the morning of her birthday meeting with them, they'd damn well better be waiting for her to show up. She backed out of the driveway after hitting send and followed Rayshawn's Audi out of their cul de sac.

****

Rain was beginning to sprinkle Jaicyn's windshield as she sat inside the warm car waiting for Rayshawn to finish unloading ten plastic storages bins from the U-Haul truck and store them safely inside their climate controlled storage unit. She tried to help him but then it started raining. Jaicyn didn't care how many hundreds of thousands of dollars worth of drugs were in those bins. She wasn't getting her hair wet.

Jaicyn and Rayshawn's re-up came directly from Cesar every two months like clockwork; one hundred kilos of raw uncut cocaine to be distributed as necessary. She and her man protected each shipment with their lives.

She powered on her iPad and pulled up the security software. From anywhere in the world, she and Rayshawn could monitor the security cameras in their house, the storage unit, and each of their stash houses.

Technology was a beautiful thing.

She checked in on her stash house. Her crew leader, Rock, and two others were doing exactly as she'd ordered, waiting for her and clueless that their boss was looking right at them and monitoring their every move.

It had taken almost a full year before the three tough guys that Jaicyn was watching on her screen had given her the respect she demanded. Rock was the worst but Jaicyn understood why. Before she came along, he was the man in Atlanta. He ran a solid crew and was making money on his own. When King had approached Rock about coming on board with the promise of tripling his profits, Rock had been under the impression that King was sending a crew to work for him.

Then Jaicyn and Rayshawn came to town and Rayshawn immediately put his girlfriend in charge of Rock and his crew of dealers in the West End. The entire five man crew went rogue as soon as Jaicyn tried to take over. They acted as if she didn't even exist and when she tried to rein them in, they called in their girlfriends.

"*Rayshawn, I have a plan*," is what she said when Rayshawn tried to take her crew away from her and put her in charge of the money again.

That was the last thing she'd wanted. She spent enough years working for Rayshawn. In her own mind, she was as much as a boss as he was and she refused to back down. Instead she hit the streets herself. Armed with the best dope Atlanta had ever seen, she hustled on street corners night and day until Rock and his boys had to take notice.

She was taking money out of their pockets; no one wanted the stepped on shit that they were selling when they could cop primo dope from her. One by one, the dealers fell back in line with her and she welcomed them with open arms. Now they all were making money and she wasn't out on corners slinging product.

Now she was finally getting the respect that she'd commanded in Washington Heights.

Jaicyn looked up from her iPad just in time to see Rayshawn motioning for her to roll down her window.

"What?" she yelled.

"Stop bullshittin' and come get your shit. I'm not packing your bags too!"

Leaving the car running, Jaicyn sprinted into the storage unit under the cover of the largest umbrella she could find in her trunk. Rayshawn tossed two black nylon gym bags at her feet and popped the lid on one of the bins. Jaicyn opened another and started packing kilos of cocaine into her bags.

"Just take five," Rayshawn said.

"I know," she muttered.

They did this at least once a week but Rayshawn always said the same thing. Her crew could sell more than five kilos in a week but Jaicyn refused to let Rayshawn know that. She always knew that she could outsell him but whenever she did, their relationship took a hit. She wanted to keep the peace so she resisted the urge and restricted her people to five kilos a week.

When the bags were tucked safely into their trunks and the unit secured, Rayshawn met Jaicyn at her car and kissed her goodbye.

"Don't be gone too long," he said. "It is your birthday."

"Be safe," she said and rolled up the window. The two black cars pulled out of the parking lot and went in opposite directions towards the city.

Jaicyn rode down I-75 blasting her music and singing along with the Jay-Z CD. Things had changed drastically in the last three years. She had changed. She had to or else her relationship wasn't going to last.

She and Rayshawn had left Washington Heights knowing what King expected from them. He wanted to expand and make more money. What they did in Atlanta was important to a lot of people back home, at least that was what Rayshawn lectured her about at least once a week.

But the hours they spent working in different parts of Atlanta took a toll on their relationship. They argued a lot.

Jaicyn shuddered, remembering the argument that had almost lost her the man she loved for good. When Rayshawn accused her of being more focused on impressing King with how much money she could make instead of making their relationship work, Jaicyn thought it was over.

Technically it was.

Rayshawn had moved out of their apartment and left her. For months he treated her like she was just another one of his employees. He'd done that before but this time it was different…much different. He didn't look at her the same. He didn't smile when she walked into his drug house in College Park. He didn't text or call her.

It broke her heart because she never thought that there would be a day when Rayshawn didn't love her anymore. He'd taught her a hard lesson and she didn't know if she was ever going to get him back. It wasn't Rayshawn, Autumn, Sandy, or King who made her see how wrong she was. It was her baby sister.

Bobbie hated the fact that Rayshawn had left and she had every right to blame Jaicyn. She was the one who reminded Jaicyn that she and Rayshawn were supposed to be a team. They were supposed to be a family and that Jaicyn was doing an awful job of being a team player. She literally accused her sister of thinking she should be at the top of the pyramid when she and Rayshawn were supposed to be the strong ones on the bottom.

Jaicyn instantly regretted putting Rickie and Bobbie on a competition cheerleading squad after hearing that, but she understood the analogy. Leave it to a ten year old to put her entire mindset into perspective with a simple cheerleading reference.

It wasn't her place to compete with Rayshawn. They came to Atlanta together, to expand King's organization. He'd done everything right. He even gave her control over half of his crew so she wouldn't feel like she worked for him and she'd taken advantage of it.

It wasn't easy getting him back, not as easy as it had been when she came home from Job Corps. Especially when she had to look him in his face and admit that she'd messed up. But Rayshawn was more important to her than anything. She wanted him more than she wanted money or her own crew. If she couldn't have him, she didn't want any of it.

Those months that they spent apart had changed Jaicyn and everybody saw it. Her own father told her that he liked the "new Jaicyn", the more cooperative, "everything doesn't have to be my way or the highway" Jaicyn. Still, no one changes overnight and Jaicyn still considered herself to be a work in progress. The best part was that Rayshawn, even though he still called her selfish and stubborn sometimes, took her back.

Three years later, they worked together and she found other things to occupy her time. Her interest in selling dope was waning so it was easy to let Rayshawn take the reins. Three years later, their relationship was stronger than it ever was before and she was extra careful about not messing it up again. Nothing was worth losing her man.

Nothing.

****

The rain had stopped by the time Jaicyn pulled in front of her main stash house. She took her umbrella with her just in case. She didn't have time to go back to the salon before her party…the party that her sisters and Rayshawn had tried to keep a secret from her. She'd pretend to act surprised when she came home but she figured out what they were up to months ago.

"Why are you so dressed up?" Rock asked when she walked through the door of the small house and tossed her umbrella on the floor.

Rock, Craig, and Gary were sitting in the living room. They'd just finished a blunt. The weed smell still lingered in the air.

"You better not have been smoking my shit," Jaicyn said. "And my clothes are none of your business." She looked around the scarcely furnished room. "Where are the girls?"

"They're on the way," Gary answered. "Kayla's car wouldn't start so they had to take the bus."

Jaicyn laughed. How the three girls Rock hired to cook his dope got to the house didn't matter to her. One day of cooking dope for Rock paid enough to buy a new car. If Kayla was too stupid to figure that out instead of driving around Atlanta in a Honda with a bad engine, that was her problem.

"Well, your stuff is in the car," Jaicyn said. "I'd stay and chill with you but I have shit to do. It's my birthday."

Craig laughed. "We know. You've been talking about it for a week. You don't want to have a birthday blunt with us?"

"Seriously, that's all you can manage? A birthday blunt? As much as I pay you, y'all should be throwin' me a party at Crucial or something."

"We don't party with the boss, remember?" Craig reminded her. "Rayshawn's rules, ya know."

Jaicyn remembered her man's rules…all of them. He was right though. No matter how long they'd been selling dope for her, this crew wasn't made up of close friends like she'd had back home. And Rayshawn's first rule was "trust no one".

On her birthday, she wished she was back home with a crew that she trusted with her life and could party with. Johnny, Taylor, and Joy were her best friends and she missed them. If they had come to Atlanta with her, they wouldn't be doing drug business on her birthday. They'd hit the hottest club for a huge birthday bash.

She couldn't and wouldn't hang out with this crew. She only trusted them enough to sell drugs for her and that was stretching it. These were the same guys who wanted her dead three years ago. Money made people see things differently and they were making a lot of money. Their relationship was strictly business and would continue to be that way until Rayshawn or King said otherwise.

With all of her real friends in Washington Heights, Jaicyn tried to think of who would be at the party tonight. Of course Dayshawn would be there. He lived in the city. Her girls from *Caliente* would probably show up.

Caliente was the result of Rayshawn's second rule; *have a legit source of income*. The best advice King had passed on to Rayshawn and Jaicyn was to filter all of their money through businesses to avoid the suspicion of the IRS. Rayshawn owned the storage facility and moving company they used. He gave her a choice. It was either utilize her real estate license and get a real job or open a business. Jaicyn chose to open a business. *Caliente* was Jaicyn's upscale clothing boutique in Buckhead.

Toya and Renee ran the shop for her and they were as close real friends Jaicyn had in Atlanta. The three of them spent a lot of time together in the store and neither girl knew that Jaicyn was one of the biggest dealers in the game. She had too much to lose if she told them. Like her friends, Joy and Taylor, Renee and Toya couldn't keep a secret to save their lives.

When Kayla and her sisters arrived at the house, Jaicyn gave the same instructions she gave them every week; "don't change the recipe and don't overcook my shit" then left.

She had a party to get ready for, even if it was just her and her family.

CHAPTER 2

It was dark when Jaicyn pulled into the cul de sac. She hadn't meant to stay away from home for so long but Toya had sent her an emergency text message that something was wrong at the boutique. It turned out to be a ploy. Nothing was wrong at the shop. The girls just wanted to have lunch with their boss and make sure she was glammed up for her party.

Toya had been working on her first collection called "Ethnic Lady" and the first thing she designed was Jaicyn's gold satin party dress. The shimmer of the satin made her highlights stand out even more and the green flecks in her hazel eyes more prominent. Paired with a sick pair of Dolce heels and the diamond necklace Rayshawn had given her for Valentine's Day, Jaicyn looked like she was on her way to a photo shoot instead of a party at her house.

Jaicyn parked her car and walked into the house from the attached garage. She was too busy texting Rock to notice that her house was completely dark. Her heels stopped clicking on the marble tile as soon as she reached the foyer. Something was wrong.

The house was too quiet for a party. And too dark. Not a single light was on. Not even an upstairs bathroom light. Rayshawn and the girls never remembered to turn off all the lights.

"Rayshawn?" Jaicyn called from the foyer.

When he didn't answer, she squinted her eyes to adjust to the complete darkness. When her eyes adjusted, Jaicyn could make out shadows moving around in the living room. She immediately reached for the Glock in her purse. Before she could shoot anyone, the lights in the living room came on, filling the foyer with a bright glow and a shout of "Surprise" from twenty of her closest friends and family. Jaicyn nearly peed on herself in her new dress.

"Oh my God!" she gushed over and over as she recognized the friends from Washington Heights that she hadn't seen in years. Everyone she missed was standing in her living room.

Autumn, Johnny, Joy, Taylor…even Blaque and Corey had made the trip to Atlanta.

"How did you do this?" Jaicyn asked Rayshawn. He smiled smugly and pointed to her sisters. Rickie and Bobbie grinned proudly.

"It's the least we could do," Rickie answered. "Grandma Juanita helped."

"My grandmother's here?" Jaicyn spun on her heels and surveyed the crowd. She couldn't believe her eyes. Standing right next to her father was Juanita, smiling and glowing, fresh off a plane from Puerto Rico.

Jaicyn hadn't seen her grandmother since she moved to Atlanta. She was so busy with her "businesses" and taking care of her sisters that she couldn't just go to Puerto Rico and visit, no matter how bad she wanted to.

"Don't cry baby-girl," Juanita said as she hugged her only grandchild. "You'll mess up all that pretty makeup."

"I'm so happy to see you," Jaicyn cried anyway. "And you brought Daddy with you. I thought he was still mad at me."

"I don't hold grudges that long," Jason grinned at his only child. "I've learned that you're going to do whatever the hell you want to, no matter what I say."

From Miami, Jason Castillo had watched his daughter make one bad choice after another. He hated what she did to make money but was powerless to stop her. He tried though. Until she gave up the game and put her intelligence to work doing something positive, he'd never stop.

"I hate to break up the family reunion," Rayshawn said, "but the party is downstairs."

Jaicyn followed her boyfriend down to their completely furnished basement and paused at bottom of the steps. Their basement had been transformed into a nightclub! Complete with a DJ, a bar, and a disco ball. Jaicyn laughed.

"What is this?"

"You're always bragging about how much fun you have at the club," Bobbie said. "And we can't get into a club so we decided to bring the club here."

Jaicyn couldn't contain the smile that stretched across her face. At twelve and thirteen, Bobbie and Rickie would never see the inside of the Velvet Room or Club Crucial. The idea to transform the basement into a nightclub they could get into was pure genius!

"This is amazing," Jaicyn said to her sisters. She had tears in her eyes.

"Don't cry, Jay-Jay," Bobbie said and wrapped her arms around Jaicyn's waist. "You'll mess up your dress."

"Yeah," Rickie co-signed. "Grandma Juanita cooked all the food too and we haven't eaten yet. No one wants to wait for you to change."

Laughing, Jaicyn followed her little sisters to the area they had roped off with real velvet ropes.

"This is the VIP section," Bobbie explained. "You like it?"

Jaicyn nodded and eyed the six foot table piled high with her favorite foods. Her stomach growled in anticipation of what was to come. She was in awe, especially when she saw the table piled high with birthday gifts.

"Here you go, baby," Rayshawn said. He handed her a glass of champagne and kissed her on the cheek. "Happy Birthday."

"How did you manage to get the entire Oak Park crew down here?" she whispered.

"I just made the call," he said. "They're your friends, Jay-Jay. All they needed was an invitation to come."

"Can I get a picture with the birthday girl?" Autumn interrupted. Jaicyn wrapped her arms around her best friend and hugged her tightly.

"I cannot believe you're here!" she squealed. "You never take off work!"

Autumn was one of three high school guidance counselors in Cincinnati. She worked way past the final bell and went to school at night. She'd be finished with her Master's program in a few more months and Jaicyn couldn't wait. Autumn was moving to Atlanta as soon as she got her degree…hopefully.

"I've missed your last two birthdays," Autumn said. "I wasn't missing a third. You come to Cincinnati for my birthday every year. It's the least I could do."

"Don't lie," Jaicyn laughed. "You know you just wanted to see Dayshawn."

"I can see him anytime. What I can't do is see my best friend any time I want to."

Jaicyn squeezed her friend again. "I'm so happy you're here. Let's eat. By the time I'm done, this dress is not going to fit!"

Autumn eyed the form fitting dress and shook her head. "It barely fits now. One empanada and you're done for."

****

A few hours later Jaicyn's birthday party was still going strong. She loved being the center of attention. She felt incredibly special that so many of the people she missed so much had taken the time out of their lives to come to Atlanta and spend her birthday with her.

Jaicyn wasn't completely drunk yet but was well on her way. She had to keep up with her man. She was sitting on the leather couch in the "VIP" while Rayshawn rubbed her leg and kept whispering that he wanted everyone to go so they could finish the party in their bedroom when Jason and Juanita came over to say goodnight.

"Happy Birthday, baby-girl," Jason said and kissed his daughter on her forehead.

"You're leaving?"

"*Si*," Juanita answered. "It's late. We're going to go back to the hotel. Do you want us to take Rickie and Bobbie with us?"

Jaicyn glanced at her sisters who were sitting on another couch about to fall asleep.

"Might as well," Jaicyn answered. "They don't have school tomorrow. And I'd really like to have the night alone," she smirked, "if you know what I mean."

"Everyone knows what you mean, Jaicyn," her father answered. "You don't have to elaborate."

Jaicyn walked over to her sisters and nudged both of them.

"Hey, wake up. Go pack an overnight bag so you can go to the hotel with Daddy."

"Right now?" Rickie whined. "But we haven't done the cake yet."

"Let's do it now," Juanita said. "I'll get the cake."

The girls quickly jumped up from the couch and ran to the DJ booth. The music shut off and the party became quiet as Juanita rolled the biggest chocolate cake Jaicyn had ever seen into the room. It was glowing from the twenty-four flaming gold candles.

"Hang on everybody," Rickie announced, with the DJ's microphone in her hand. At thirteen Rickie was very mature but she looked nervous standing in front of so many people. Bobbie stood next to her and Jaicyn listened intently, wondering what they were going to say.

"We just want to thank everyone for coming tonight to help us celebrate our sister's birthday," Rickie said to the crowd.

"And we have a few things we'd like to say to our big sister," Bobbie added and looked at Jaicyn.

"Jay-Jay, Rickie and I know that we don't say thank you enough and often take a lot of the stuff you do for us for granted. But I remember living in our apartment in Washington Heights and how you always made sure we had food and cable so we could watch cartoons. We didn't have much but you always made sure we were okay even when our own mother didn't care about us."

"Even when we had to go to that foster home," Rickie said, "we knew that you'd figure out a way to bring us all together. We know that you work hard to give us things and Rayshawn spoils you."

Everyone in the room laughed as Jaicyn fingered the diamond necklace around her neck and Rayshawn nodded guiltily.

"But we never do anything super special for you," Rickie continued. "That's why we wanted to give you a good party. We love you Big Sis. Happy Birthday." Rickie hugged her sister tightly and whispered "Thank you".

Jaicyn held both her sisters' hands as Autumn stepped forward and began singing a heart stopping rendition of Happy Birthday. Autumn's voice was absolutely amazing. Jaicyn could have cried when it was over but she didn't have time. Rayshawn took the microphone from Autumn and started speaking.

"Before we dive into that enormous cake, there's something that I want to say."

The crowd hushed. Jaicyn stared at Rayshawn trying to figure out what he was up to.

"We've been together for nine years," Rayshawn said to Jaicyn. "We've been through some shit that I don't need to mention but the point is, we made it through and we did it together. I made a promise to you when we were sixteen. My boys laughed at that silly little ring I gave you but you wear it every day because it means something serious."

Rayshawn reached into his pocket and pulled out a ring, a sparkling five carat pear shaped solitaire set in platinum. Jaicyn's breath caught in her throat.

"Jay-Jay, I gave you that ring as a promise that I made to one day make you my wife. And I'm a man of my word. I want to make good on that promise today."

Rayshawn took Jaicyn's left hand and slid the gold band off of her finger. He got down on one knee and looked up at his girlfriend.

"Jaicyn, will you marry me?"

Jaicyn was speechless and too choked up to say anything anyway. All she could do was nod her head yes. Behind Jaicyn, her father beamed as Rayshawn slipped the new ring on her finger and the guests clapped and cheered.

Jaicyn couldn't believe that Rayshawn had actually proposed to her and did it in front of so many people. That was totally out of the norm for him. As she stared down at the shimmering diamond she got excited. Rayshawn was finally ready to get married! She would have married him years ago but waited patiently until he was ready. There was nothing in the world that Jaicyn wanted more than to be Mrs. Rayshawn Moore and it was finally happening.

CHAPTER 3

A loud bang that sounded like a flurry of pots being dropped on marble flooring jolted Rayshawn out of his nap in the basement. He immediately reached for his phone and checked the time. It was still early. He had almost two hours before he had to pick up King from the airport.

Atlanta was King's first stop on his three city check-ins. Usually he checked in on Rayshawn and Jaicyn after flying out to L.A. to check on Slim and ended his trip in New York to look in on Blaque. But the only ones with anything new going on were Jaicyn and Rayshawn so he decided to see them first.

Rayshawn rolled off the sofa and walked heavily up the stairs. Lately he'd been so tired. His shoulders were heavy and tense as he made his way up the stairs. He clenched his teeth harder than they already where. Rickie and Bobbie's laughter was making his head hurt.

Jaicyn knew he'd had a long night. She knew when he walked in their bedroom at three in the morning and passed out on top of the covers. Now his day was going to be even longer than last night because King was coming. Why couldn't she keep her sisters quiet for one damn hour?

"What the hell are y'all doin'?" Rayshawn yelled at Rickie and Bobbie.

"We're making cupcakes for our cheerleading squad," Rickie answered.

Rayshawn took one glance around the kitchen and knew that they weren't making just cupcakes. Making a straight up mess was more accurate. Sugar, flour, and cupcake batter was all over the counters and floor. And the cupcakes...well they looked like nothing but dark brown lumps and definitely not edible.

"Where is your sister?"

"You mean your *wife*?" Bobbie teased.

Rayshawn grinned. "Shut up. Where is she?"

"I don't know. She said she had errands to run."

"You better hope those errands included picking you up some cupcakes," Rayshawn joked. "No one is going to eat those."

"Get out of here!" Rickie eased across the kitchen with her flour covered hands stretched out in front of her. Rayshawn jumped back a few steps to avoid her flour handprints on his new jeans and sweater. He grabbed his ATL fitted cap off the counter before it was ruined too and slipped it on his head.

"I'm going to make some runs. Don't burn down my house and tell your sister to call me when she gets home."

"Don't you mean tell my wife to call when she gets home," Bobbie laughed.

Rayshawn rolled his eyes at the two girls and left the kitchen.

Rickie and Bobbie, along with every other female he knew was straight up giddy that he finally proposed to Jaicyn. Any time someone said *wedding*, they'd burst out in high pitched giggles and plead with Jaicyn to show them her ring again.

What is it with females and weddings? Rayshawn thought to himself as he walked to his car. They all acted the same way when Sandy married King. All they cared about was the wedding. No one seemed too concerned about the marriage.

Who cares about the wedding? Rayshawn didn't even want a wedding. He'd be perfectly happy going to Vegas and getting hitched at the Little White Wedding Chapel in his jeans and t-shirt. The marriage was the most important thing.

Being married and acting like a wife was the commitment he wanted from Jaicyn, not the chance for her to be the center of attention. The last thing his girlfriend needed was more attention. With the huge house she had to have, the expensive clothes, shoes, and jewelry she couldn't get enough of, the flashy cars, and her celebrity clients at the shop, Jaicyn got more than enough attention.

Maybe getting married and popping out a couple of kids would settle her down some. That's what Rayshawn hoped for. Maybe, just maybe, she'd realize that it was time for her to take a step back and get out the game before her need for attention brought them the kind of attention that they didn't need. Like from the FEDS.

The two of them were playing a dangerous game. The only time Jaicyn ever thought about how dangerous the drug game could be was when she had to fight with other crews trying to steal her product or her workers. She ignored the fact they had legit money coming in but damn sure not enough to afford the lifestyle that they lived. *Caliente* wasn't that hot!

Somebody was sure to start noticing and paying a little more attention to the twenty-four year olds living in a house that cost almost a half million dollars and driving better cars than their rich doctor and lawyer neighbors. Someone was bound to ask how they could afford to send Rickie and Bobbie to private school if Rayshawn had caved to what Jaicyn wanted and actually sent them.

"We run this city," Jaicyn had said when she showed him the house. "So what if we spend some of our money on a house. We deserve it."

She did deserve the house and much more, but Rayshawn was hesitant to show that kind of money just three years after moving to Atlanta. Their come up was too fast. They both needed to slow down. One day Jaicyn would have to start listening to him. Maybe King could talk some sense into her.

****

Rayshawn inched his Audi forward two feet, waiting for the trio of elderly tourists to hurry and pack their luggage into the trunk of the taxi. His rap music blaring from his open windows made them move a little faster. Through his dark shades, Rayshawn scanned the sidewalk for King. His plane had landed over thirty minutes ago. Rayshawn was about to pull off and circle the airport one more time when he spotted King walking through the automatic doors dragging his Louis Vuitton carry-on behind him. Even fresh off a plane, King walked like he owned the world. His perfectly tailored slacks and black Dolce shirt made him hard to miss amongst the other travelers. Rayshawn rolled down the automatic window and called King's name.

"What's up youngin'?" King grinned at his protégé when he got in the car. "You finally got rid of the Camry, huh? Now you're driving a man's car."

Rayshawn laughed. "Jaicyn's idea. Still got the Camry though, for road trips, ya know."

"I taught you well."

Rayshawn pulled out of the airport seconds before an Atlanta cop could knock on his window and tell him to move his car out of the passenger pickup zone.

"So what's good?" King asked as they hit the interstate and Rayshawn edged the needle towards eighty-five miles per hour, a more suitable speed for him.

"What's good with what?" Rayshawn responded absently. He wrinkled his brow and glanced at King.

The question was a surprise. The first thing that King had ever taught anyone in his crew was not to talk business in the car.

"I meant, how's life? I heard Jay-Jay's party was off the hook."

"Yeah," Rayshawn nodded.

"Heard you popped the question too."

Rayshawn nodded again. He knew that word would have gotten back to King that he proposed. There were too many Washington Heights peeps at the party for him not to find out. Of course Sandy was one of the first people that Jaicyn called. Rayshawn wondered what King thought about him and Jaicyn getting married.

But King was silent for an uncomfortable minute. Rayshawn fidgeted in the driver's seat and pressed a little harder on the gas.

"You sure that's what you want to do?" King finally asked. "You're still young, kid. Why get married at twenty-four?"

Rayshawn simply answered, "It's time."

King leaned back against the soft leather headrest and stared at the cars that Rayshawn was leaving in the dust. Since he'd known the boy,

Rayshawn took personal advice with a grain of salt. He hung on to every single word that King said when it came to business but anything about his relationships, especially anything that had to do with Jaicyn, went in one ear and out the other.

King was prepared to do his best to talk them out of marriage, but Rayshawn's firm "It's time" put that idea right out of his mind. Instead he watched the cars that whizzed past the Audi. The Atlanta bypass made King a little leery. Dangerous drivers texting and driving, assholes crossing lanes without the use of turn signals or any form of common sense, all while exceeding the fifty-five mile an hour speed limit put everyone at risk.

"Where are we going'?" King asked when Rayshawn skipped the exit that would have led to his house.

"Thought we'd meet Dayshawn at this little jazz spot he found a few weeks ago. It's a decent spot to talk."

"Cool."

Rayshawn's phone vibrated in the center console and King laughed. It was Jaicyn.

"Does your girl have a sixth sense or something? She always calls when you're hangin' with me."

"Some things never change. She wanted to come but I told her to stay home for a change." Rayshawn pushed the ignore button.

He wasn't worried that something bad had happened to his fiancée or his house. Jaicyn knew better than to let her sisters destroy the house and the last time he talked to her, she was shopping at Lenox. The only bad thing that could happen was her running out of cash.

Thirty minutes later, Rayshawn pulled the Audi into a small parking lot, handed a bum a fifty with instructions to make sure no one came within two feet of the car, and led King into the building. Dayshawn was sitting in a corner booth watching the sexy saxophone playing seductress on stage. The girl was playing her sax so seductively it looked like she was making love to it.

"She's fine as hell," King commented as he slid into the booth.

She wasn't just fine. She was F-I-N-E!! Her slinky silver jersey dress stopped mid-thigh showing off two perfectly shapely bronze legs and clung to her hips and breasts for dear life. Her light eyes caught the light and sparkled as she blew her horn.

"Who is she?" Rayshawn asked his brother.

"I don't know, but damn!" Dayshawn said. "Is she single?"

"Autumn is going to kick your ass," Rayshawn chuckled.

He waved to a waitress, ordered a bucket of ice and a bottle of Hennessy. He didn't ask the price. Bars and clubs always marked up the price of bottles, especially in Atlanta.

The dark club and corner booth provided the men optimal privacy to discuss business matters. After being in Atlanta for so long and now making more money than ever before, Rayshawn didn't mind letting his twin in on his business.

In a few months, Dayshawn would be graduating from law school and his experience interning at a very prominent law firm in Atlanta was the reason that Jaicyn and Rayshawn stayed out of jail during the Atlanta police raids last year. Dayshawn needed to know everything that Rayshawn was into and how deep so that he knew the right questions to ask his mentors. Rayshawn paid for his education and Dayshawn used that education to protect his brother.

King watched the twins quietly as they ogled the girl on stage and jonesed each other about their girlfriends. His mouth turned up into a slight smile. Proud was too light of a word to describe how he felt about the twins. He cared about them just as much as he cared about his own son. Who knew where both of them would be if he hadn't stepped in and took Rayshawn under his wing? Definitely still in Washington Heights. Without him, they would have ended up just like their aunts and uncles.

Or their father.

"Stop checkin' out that girl," King ordered the twins and gulped down his drink. "She don't want either of you."

"You just want to get to business," Dayshawn laughed. "You know Jaicyn is cooking for you."

"Yeah," Rayshawn added. "We all know the real reason you came here first is because you miss those bad ass girls of mine. When we get to the house, I'm not gonna see you for the rest of the trip. You brought them gifts again, didn't you?"

"Not this trip," King smiled. "You and Jay-Jay spoil those girls enough. But we do need to chat a little."

"About what? Everything's good down here," Rayshawn replied with his eye still on the jazz player as she introduced her band.

"Cesar said your re-up was three hundred grand this month. What the hell is going on down here?"

A re-up that large was cause for concern. No one in King's crew was selling dope like that. Not even Slim who was doing big things in Los Angeles.

"It's Jaicyn, man," Rayshawn groaned. "Her crew sells dope like Wal-mart sells diapers. She won't slow down."

Rayshawn didn't like to admit that Jaicyn was outselling him but King had to know. Jaicyn was once again pissing off the Atlanta dealers. The last thing Rayshawn wanted was another Pete and Marcello incident. She wouldn't listen to him though.

Shooting at his fiancée was serious and Rayshawn would risk everything to make sure that Jaicyn was safe when she drove her black on black Charger through the West End or the SWATS.

All Jaicyn wanted was money. That's why she pushed her crew so hard. Rayshawn hated dealing with the financials. He hated paying taxes and keeping records. Jaicyn loved it, therefore he allowed her to do what she did best, manage the money. Jaicyn took classes on investing and channeled all of their hard earned money through their very successful businesses. She was addicted to watching the balance in their bank accounts grow.

As much as she spent, Jaicyn saved even more. Coming from a place where money was scarce had that effect on her. She never wanted to be without it again. Rayshawn knew there was some magic number, some high ass dollar amount that she was aiming for; he just didn't know what it was. But he'd do whatever he had to for her to reach that number. He'd promised her.

"How many a week can they sell?" King asked.

"Ten to twenty keys, easy," Rayshawn answered. "She's trying to be good and not go over ten, but Atlanta is big, man. This shit ain't like Washington Heights at all. Niggas down here be trippin'. They don't like her as is."

"They don't like her like Pete and Marcello didn't like her?"

"Worse," Dayshawn answered. "One of the lawyers at my firm represents a lot of dealers down here and they always have something to say about Jaicyn and Rayshawn. These cats are out here doing whatever they need to do to get money because y'all are making to hard for them. They're getting reckless and getting locked up in the process."

"Damn Rayshawn! I sent you down here to make money, not turn the city against you," King sighed.

"Don't worry about it," Rayshawn answered with a glint in his eye. "I have a plan."

King smirked. "What's your plan?"

"We can flip the script on these folks. I'm talking about wholesale," Rayshawn explained. "I'm talkin' about letting the crews do their own thing. They cop from us like we cop from Cesar. We talked about expanding into North Carolina and west to Tennessee and Alabama before. I think I could even supply some people in Florida. They're already coming up here to get shit from me."

"You tryin' to be top dog?" King raised his eyebrows. That was a ballsy move for Rayshawn to even suggest.

"I'm not tryin' to be nothin'," Rayshawn answered. "I'm trying to make things safer for me and my family. It just makes sense for us to switch up. This city is too big and there are too many dealers. They all can't work for us, not when it's just me and Jaicyn who got the good dope."

Rayshawn stared at King, hoping he understood. He needed him on his side. King was his link to Cesar and Cesar had the best dope in the game.

"How much do you think you can sell?"

Rayshawn held up five fingers.

"Seriously?" King asked.

Rayshawn nodded. "Like I said, niggas are already coming from Tennessee, Alabama, and North Carolina to get their hands on Cesar's good dope.

"How many did you say?" Dayshawn asked.

"Five hundred," Rayshawn answered.

"What's the plan? Are you going to sell it at regular wholesale prices?"

"Yeah."

Dayshawn almost spit his drink all over the table when he calculated their profits in his head. His brother was talking about millions of dollars in dope. That wasn't laying low or playing it safe.

"Whoa, Rayshawn," King held up his hand. "Slow your roll. I can't have you down here pushin' that much weight! Cesar ain't gon front you that much dope anyway. Are you crazy?"

"But I'm good for it!"

"No you're not," King said. "You and Jaicyn don't have five million dollars just lying around. We'll talk to the man and work this shit out. We'll come up with a logical number that won't have your ass in prison for the rest of your life. And don't get your panties in a bunch," King added when he saw the disappointed look on Rayshawn's face.

"I like this idea for you and Jaicyn. But we have to take our time with this. There's no rush."

To Rayshawn, the sooner they could make the transition, the better. The longer Jaicyn stayed on the streets hustling with her crew, the higher chance she had of getting shot and him going to jail. He wanted to let everyone go as soon as possible and sit back and collect the cash, like King.

Let the street hustlers fight over territory and bullshit like that. He was tired of getting his hands dirty.

"When can we talk to Cesar?" Rayshawn asked anxiously.

"I'll talk to him when I get back from New York. You just hang tight," King told him. "In the meantime, talk this over with your girl. I know you haven't said nothing about this to her because she'd be here tonight running her mouth if you had."

"She'll be cool with it," Rayshawn answered confidently. "It means more money and she's been hinting at opening another store. I don't think she wants to do this shit much longer anyway. She's really into this fashion thing now."

King nodded his head but didn't reply. Rayshawn still didn't fully understand Jaicyn, even after all these years. When it came to her, Rayshawn still lived in fantasy world. What he wanted from his girlfriend, like stability and normalcy, he'd never get.

Jaicyn liked the money, but like King, she relished in the power. If she and Rayshawn became one of the biggest dope suppliers in the south, which is what King wanted for them, Jaicyn would easily become one of the most powerful women in Atlanta. She wouldn't give that up in order to stay home and have Rayshawn's babies.

"Speaking of Jaicyn," King spoke up. "I think you should know that Ramel is out."

"He's out? Like for good?"

King poured another glass of Hennessy. "Yeah. Surprisingly, he's out early for good behavior."

"Fuck!" Rayshawn uttered.

His mind when straight back to the night he found out that Jaicyn had been raped and beaten by Ramel and his uncle, Mario. Heat raced through his body and his hand clenched the cool glass of liquor.

Jaicyn, lying in her hospital bed, covered in bandages, had been barely recognizable. It had taken months for her body to heal. She never talked about what happened. Not to anyone.

Back then, Rayshawn hadn't wanted to hear the details and deliberately stayed away when Jaicyn gave her deposition to the cops and prosecutor. She was still in the hospital when Ramel's court date came, thanks to King's campaign contribution to the DA who pushed Ramel's case to the top of the pile. She was able to give her testimony via videotape that was played in court.

After Ramel was sentenced to ten years Jaicyn went on with her life and acted like it never happened. Rayshawn promised her that if she ever wanted to talk about it, he'd listen. But she never did. Ramel being locked up probably helped her cope. He didn't know how Jaicyn would take the news about Ramel walking the streets of Washington Heights. She'd probably freak out a little bit. Ramel knew that Rayshawn killed Mario. He knew when it happened. And Ramel Cruz had 2,920 days to plot his revenge. The Cruz family lived by the same code as Rayshawn.

Don't fuck with family.

"Should I be worried?" Rayshawn asked King.

"No. Ramel's just talking shit right now. He's fresh from the pen. It's going to take him a minute to build up his crew and get strong enough to come at us."

"Besides," Dayshawn said, "you don't have a reason to be in Washington Heights anyway. Ramel isn't coming down here, I guarantee it."

They were both right. Rayshawn took a swig from his drink and cherished the feel of the smooth cold liquor burning its way down his throat. He liked having Dayshawn and King around. They were always the voice of reason.

"Look," he finally said. "Let's just leave this between us. I don't think I want Jay-Jay to know yet."

"Agreed," King said. "Let's get this shit with Cesar worked out before we have your girl coming to Washington Heights all guns ablazin' and shit and getting us all killed."

"Good idea," Dayshawn laughed as he slid out of the booth.

"Where you goin'?" Rayshawn demanded. He looked in the direction his twin was headed.

"Gotta find out where I can get that girl's...CD," Dayshawn laughed.

"Hurry up. We're about to go!" Rayshawn yelled at his brother's back.

"Negro, I drove my own car. Leave whenever you feel like it."

"Don't cock block, Rayshawn," King admonished. "Him and Autumn aren't even that serious. Let him do his thing. That girl is bad and not every twenty-four year old is rushing down the aisle like you."

Rayshawn rolled his eyes in his head and gave one last glance at the sax player. She was pretty but he already had the baddest chick in Atlanta in his bed. Jaicyn could out dress, out talk, and outshine every woman that Rayshawn had ever come in contact with. He had a diamond at home. A diamond wearing his diamond and all he wanted was her.

CHAPTER 4

Fifth, sixth, and seventh graders rushed out of Stone Mountain Middle School as soon as the final bell signaled they were free to go. The mass exodus of pre-teens rushing to waiting parents and school buses made Jaicyn fidget against her car door. Some of the kids were friends of her sisters but none of their parents were friends of hers. None of them congratulated her on her huge diamond engagement ring. They simply turned away from the flashy young lady who spoiled her sisters so much that *their* children were jealous, demanding iPhones and designer clothes because Rickie and Bobbie had them.

Fuck it, Jaicyn thought to herself. *I don't feel like dealing with these broke bitches anyway.*

So what if she bought her sisters Gucci, Juicy Couture, and Betsy Johnson while the other kids got Old Navy jeans and GAP shirts. Why should Rickie and Bobbie settle for cheering for a middle school football team when they could be on the best competition squad in the state? Nothing but the best for them. Jaicyn made sure of it.

She wouldn't have to deal with jealous ass parents who couldn't afford the things she could if Rayshawn would just say yes to private

34

school. The fashion conscious sisters wouldn't stand out so much if everyone else had what they had.

Rayshawn was convinced that private school was unnecessary. The schools in Georgia were much better than the Washington Heights public schools that they'd gone to. Besides, how would they explain how they were able to afford the tuition? The school that Jaicyn had her eye on was twenty grand a year, per student. There was no way that they could explain how they were able to pay for the girls to go to that school without raising suspicions.

Jaicyn spotted her sisters walking towards her and moved around her car to the driver's side. She smiled in approval of Rickie and Bobbie's thin sweater dresses and tights. Like she did at thirteen, the girls were starting to develop bodies that attracted a lot of attention. Rickie was already filling up a B-cup. By summer, Jaicyn was sure she'd be in a C. Kids' sizes didn't even fit the girls anymore. It was definitely time to start teaching them about boys and sex, something her own mother never found the time to do.

Jaicyn didn't want her sisters having sex. She wanted them to wait. When all her friends in Washington Heights were having sex and having babies in high school, Jaicyn stuck by her "no sex" policy. Holding out had gotten her more than babies. Boys with after school jobs and other sources of income were happy to shower her with clothes, shoes, and jewelry in hopes of being her first. She used them for what they would give her so she could use the money she made from stealing clothes to take care of her sisters.

Closed legs don't get fed was bullshit. Spreading her legs to Jason, Ricky, and Bobby hadn't helped Angelina Jones feed her daughters. Jaicyn had even made Rayshawn wait a year before she gave him some.

He was her first and only. Look at them now! She had everything she wanted and a wedding to plan!

"Is your name Jaicyn?" a tall skinny girl in a fake leather jacket and knock off Chanel sunglasses said to Jaicyn.

Jaicyn adjusted her Jackie O Ray Bans and gave the girl a quick onceover. Jaicyn had never seen the girl before and the scowl on her face told Jaicyn that the skinny girl wasn't hanging around to compliment her on her ring.

"Who wants to know?" Jaicyn answered. She glanced in the car where her brand new pink and black .22 was sitting in a box on the backseat. Damn it! If the girl tried something, Jaicyn would be forced to beat the bitch down with her fists. She calmly ran her hands over her left bra strap feeling for the box cutter she kept there…just in case.

"So, are you Jaicyn?" the girl said.

"Like I said, who wants to know?" Jaicyn repeated.

Out of the corner of her eye she saw Rickie and Bobbie stop walking. She made a slight gesture with her hand to let them know to hurry up and get to the car. If she needed to get away quickly, she didn't want to have to wait for them.

"I have a message for you," the girl paused. "From D-train."

Jaicyn scrambled to remember who D-train was. The name sounded familiar but she couldn't register it.

"Who?"

"Bitch, don't act like you don't know who the fuck I'm talking about!" the girl yelled. "D-train said you better stay out of the SWATS! Moore Street is his and if he sees you down there again, he's goin' to fuck you up!"

"Really?" Jaicyn laughed. "Tell you what. You go back to Moore Street and tell D-train that I said if he wants to make money in the SWATS he better come work for me. And make sure you tell him that if he sends another raggedy bitch with a message for me, I'm gonna fuck him up!"

"Fuck you!"

The girl swung her fist wildly at Jaicyn, catching her on the shoulder when Jaicyn backed up a few inches so she wouldn't hit her face. She grabbed the girl's cheap weave with one hand and pulled her box cutter with the other. She held the blade against the girl's throat, pressing just hard enough to let the girl know she was serious.

"Bitch, I will slice your fuckin' throat if you ever put your hands on me again. You got beef with me; we'll handle that shit in the SWATS. Don't you ever come up to this school again."

Jaicyn punched the skinny girl in her stomach and pushed her away from the car. Seconds later, Rickie and Bobbie got in the car laughing as Jaicyn peeled out of the parking lot.

"Shut up!" she yelled at them. "That shit ain't funny! I can't have bitches coming up to your school looking for me. This is bullshit!" Jaicyn pounded her fists against the steering wheel.

Rickie and Bobbie didn't utter another word for the rest of the way home. As soon they got home they ran to find Rayshawn. He walked into the bedroom where Jaicyn was slipping into a pair of jeans. Her skirt was in a heap on the floor and her favorite Prada sling backs were kicked across the room.

"What are you doing?" he asked calmly. Jaicyn didn't answer. She opened her dresser drawer and pulled out some socks then slipped on a pair of sneakers. Her black hoodie was zipped all the way up.

"Jaicyn!"

"What?" she snapped angrily.

"What are you doing?"

"Call the fellas," she demanded. "We're going over to Moore Street and find this nigga D-train and fuck him up. How he gon send some wack ass bitch up to my sisters' school to give me a message. You know I don't play that shit, Rayshawn!" She positioned her box cutter underneath her bra strap and tucked her other gun into her waistband.

"Why are you still standing there?"

"Baby, calm down. We're not goin' to just mount up and start blastin' niggas we don't know. You know that's not how we handle shit. Who's this dude anyway?"

"The hell if I know," Jaicyn yelled. "Just some reckless ass idiot that's pissed off that he can't get no money in the SWATS." She tried to move past Rayshawn to leave the room but he blocked the door.

"Jaicyn, for real, calm down. We have people that handle this type of shit! Let me find out what's going on and I'll get Chris and Ronnie on it," Rayshawn said, naming the two people he hired to take care of people like D-train.

"You better do something quick," Jaicyn mumbled.

Rayshawn shook his head and walked out of the bedroom. King needed to hurry up and get back to him about Cesar. The sooner he could get Jaicyn off the streets, the better he'd sleep at night.

****

Jaicyn's temper still hadn't subsided hours later after she made dinner and was watching Jay-Z's "Answer the Call" concert on YouTube. She paused the show when Autumn's face appeared on her caller ID. She pressed the speakerphone button.

"What's up girl?"

"Are you sitting down?" Autumn asked anxiously.

"Yeah. What's up?"

"You will never guess who I saw when I was in Washington Heights with my parents earlier."

Autumn knew that Jaicyn hadn't heard the news yet or she would have called Autumn by now. Word on the street was that Ramel Cruz had been home for months and the only thing on his mind was finding Rayshawn and Jaicyn.

"Who?" Jaicyn asked absently, thinking it had to be someone they went to school with…or her mother. Even though she had told Autumn to stop looking around Washington Heights for Angelina, Autumn still did from time to time. Jaicyn hoped that Autumn wasn't going to tell her that she'd seen Angelina. It would be hard to explain to Rickie and Bobbie, especially since they thought their mother was dead.

"Ramel."

The blood drained from Jaicyn's face as her laptop crashed to the floor. Instinctively she rubbed her shoulder, where Ramel had dislocated it trying to pull her out of his car.

"No," Jaicyn whispered. "How?"

"I didn't talk to him," Autumn answered. "I heard that he's looking for you and Rayshawn but I'm sure Marcus and Corey will take care of him."

Jaicyn didn't say anything. Fear clenched her heart. If Ramel found her, raping and beating her wouldn't be enough. He'd kill her this time, probably after he raped her again. Tears streamed down Jaicyn's face as her heart pounded in her chest.

"Jay-Jay, are you there?"

Jaicyn quickly wiped her eyes with the back of her hand. "Yeah Autumn. I'll call you back, okay?"

"Jay-Jay..." Autumn was worried about her friend. Her voice was shaky. It was the first time Autumn had ever heard Jaicyn sound afraid of Ramel.

"I'm okay," Jaicyn insisted. "I just need a minute. I'll call you back." She disconnected the call before Autumn could respond. She heard footsteps headed towards the study and she quickly locked the door.

Rayshawn wiggled the knob, surprised to find the door locked.

"Jaicyn! What are you doing in there?"

She didn't want Rayshawn to see her like this, crying and afraid. She wiped her face with her shirt and smoothed her hair with her fingers. Then she unlocked the door.

"Sorry. I was on the phone with my dad," she said in a rushed voice. "We were talking about Rickie's birthday party and I didn't want her nosy ass to hear."

"Well, are you coming to bed?"

The way he asked, the hopeful lust in his question made Jaicyn cringe a little. As soon as she thought about making love to her man, she found herself back in abandoned crackhouse, with salty tears and blood stinging her eyes as Ramel and his uncle forced themselves on her, taking turns until she'd passed out from the pain. She trembled when Rayshawn touched her shoulder.

"Baby, what's wrong?"

She had to tell him. He had to know what was causing the fear in her eyes and nausea in her stomach. She'd never turned down sex with him before. He'd get upset if she started now, with no explanation.

"Umm," Jaicyn stammered, "umm, Ramel's out of jail and-"

"Yeah, I know," Rayshawn interrupted.

Jaicyn stepped back and looked at her man in surprise. How the hell did he know?

"What? You knew? When did you find out?"

Rayshawn shuffled from side to side. He knew that she'd be upset that he didn't tell her but he was still trying to figure out if he needed to do something about Ramel before telling Jaicyn.

"King told me," he replied, not willing to admit *when* King had told him. From the high angry pitch of her voice, if Jaicyn knew that Rayshawn had been keeping a secret that big for over a month, she'd probably slap the shit out of him.

"Why didn't you tell me? Why did I have to hear it from Autumn?"

"Because Autumn has a big mouth and got to you first," was his reply.

Jaicyn stood in front of him with her hands on her hips, searching his face for any sign of deception. When she couldn't find any, she turned around and walked back to the sofa. Rayshawn followed her.

"Are you okay?"

Jaicyn nodded her head, afraid that even a slight quiver in her voice would crack her façade.

"You don't have to worry about him, Jay-Jay. Ramel is weak right now. He doesn't have the muscle to come after us. If he steps out of bounds, Corey and Blaque will handle him."

Jaicyn raised her eyebrows. "Blaque? I thought he was in New York."

"Shit was getting too hot. Niggas were getting popped by the FEDS. Blaque kept his shit tight but King wasn't taking any chances and brought him back to Washington Heights."

"Oh," was all Jaicyn said. Her mind was still focused on Ramel.

Just because Blaque was in Washington Heights didn't mean that everything was kosher. Ramel could easily hop on a Greyhound and come to Atlanta. Jaicyn knew that she had to be on guard and keep her ear to the streets in Atlanta and Washington Heights.

The minute Ramel left, she would know. This time she wasn't waiting on Blaque, King, or Rayshawn to make a move.

If or when Ramel Cruz set foot in Atlanta, Georgia, Jaicyn was going to blow his head off. She would not be afraid. She'd do whatever she had to do to never feel that kind of fear again.

CHAPTER 5

"Sure Tina," Jaicyn said to the fashion conscious middle aged woman standing at the counter. "Tell your daughter to bring some samples by the next time she's in town. I'll be happy to find a place for her line in the shop."

As the woman left, Jaicyn looked around her small boutique. The store was packed with women trying on clothes and jewelry. Only five more days until the Fourth of July and the fashionistas of Atlanta were gearing up for the holiday.

Jaicyn should have been shopping for her own party but Rayshawn had insisted that she started spending more time at *Caliente*, at least until he got a handle on the situation in the SWATS.

Jaicyn had tried to sneak over there a couple times. She was losing money left and right since D-train had become such a problem. He was trying to run off her crew and her boys were nervous. D-train was a trigger happy asshole. He and his crew were making southwest Atlanta too hot. Police had begun driving through the area more frequently which meant nobody was making enough money.

Jaicyn wanted to shoot D-train right in his face for being such a problem and almost did when his crew did a quick drive-by in front of her stash house and riddled her freshly painted Charger with AK47 rounds. It took an act of God and Rayshawn hiding all of her guns to keep her from going after him.

The man was clever too. He knew how to keep a low profile when shit got too hot. Rayshawn didn't know what part of Atlanta he was hiding out in but he wasn't going to stop looking for him. D-train had to come out of hiding soon.

Jaicyn quickly tired of watching other people shop and the two sales clerks fussing over them. She picked up the latest issue of Cosmo and sat down in one of the plus chairs. She started flipping absently through the pages. She was too high-strung to concentrate on anything.

She looked up when her sisters, fresh from cheerleading camp and still in their practice clothes, walked into the boutique.

"What are you two doing here?" Jaicyn questioned. Rayshawn was supposed to have picked them up and taken them home.

"We took the train," Rickie answered.

"I didn't ask how you got here," Jaicyn said. "I asked why you're here."

Rickie and Bobbie shrugged their shoulders.

"We waited for Rayshawn but he didn't show up," Rickie explained. "So we came here to wait for you."

Jaicyn couldn't believe her ears. She didn't ask Rayshawn to do a lot for her sisters. All she asked was that he pick them up from practice every once in awhile.

"What? Did you call him?"

"Yeah," Rickie answered and plopped down on the other chair. Bobbie went off in search of new jewelry to try on.

"His phone kept going straight to voicemail," Rickie said. "I left two messages and we waited for a half hour. Then we caught the train here."

Jaicyn pulled her phone out of her pocket and called her fiancé. Like Rickie said, the call went straight to voicemail. She tried a few more times, growing more agitated each time the voicemail picked up. What could he possibly be doing? His phone was never off.

Something was wrong, seriously wrong.

"Bobbie," Jaicyn shouted. "Grab my purse from behind the counter and let's go!"

The girls had to jog to keep up with Jaicyn as she ran to her brand new Lexus, the replacement she was forced to get after D-train shot up her car.

"Jay-Jay, what's wrong?" Bobbie asked as the car peeled out of the gravel parking lot and raced down the street. Jaicyn's wrinkled brow and white knuckles as she clenched the steering wheel caused both girls to be alarmed.

Jaicyn drove like a bat out of hell through their sub-division. Something had happened to Rayshawn and as hard as she tried, she couldn't push the horrible scenarios out of her mind. Her heartbeat quickened when she pulled into their driveway next to Rayshawn's car.

Just because his car was there didn't mean that he was okay. She hopped out of the car and ran through the house frantically calling his name. She ran through each room upstairs but there was no sign of her man.

She leaned against the doorway of their bedroom and tried to calm her panicked nerves.

"Jaicyn," Rickie called upstairs, "he's outside by the pool."

Jaicyn ran through the kitchen and stopped by the sliding patio door.

Rayshawn was sitting on one of the patio chairs, his ball cap that rarely left his head, was sitting on the glass table. Jaicyn slid open the patio door, and rushed over to her fiancé. Bobbie started to follow but Rickie stopped her.

Jaicyn slowed her pace and walked over to Rayshawn. She could see that he was distraught. Something bad had happened!

Rayshawn's face and red t-shirt were wet with tears. Jaicyn had never seen him like that before and she didn't know how to approach him. All she knew was that she wasn't mad anymore. She was just relieved that he was alive.

"Rayshawn," Jaicyn said softly. Rayshawn didn't respond. Jaicyn walked over to him and put her arm around him which only made him cry harder.

"Baby, what's wrong?"

Unable to speak, Rayshawn put his head on the table. His shoulders shook as he tried to stop his tears. Jaicyn knelt down on her knee beside him. The only thing that could make Rayshawn break down like that was if something had happened to Dayshawn. Her heart sank.

"Rayshawn, baby, please tell me what happened," Jaicyn pleaded, but he still didn't say anything. Jaicyn's phone rang. She wasn't going to answer until she saw it was Little Man. He would know what was wrong with Rayshawn.

"Hello," Jaicyn said into her phone.

"Jay-Jay, where's Rayshawn?" Little Man asked.

"He's right here." Jaicyn didn't like the sound of Little Man's voice.

"Talk to me, Little Man. What's going on?"

"King got shot," he answered. "He might not make it."

"What?" Jaicyn screamed. "What are you talking about?"

"He got shot," Little Man repeated. "Him and Blaque, but Blaque is going to be okay. No disrespect Jaicyn, but I need to talk to Rayshawn."

With both King and Blaque shot down, the crew would turn to Rayshawn for their next move. But one look at her man and Jaicyn knew that he wasn't ready to deal with them.

"Look, hang back for a minute," Jaicyn instructed, taking charge of the situation. "We're on our way to the airport now."

Without waiting for a response, Jaicyn hung up her phone and shoved it back in her pocket. She walked over to the patio door and slid it open. Rickie and Bobbie jumped back, afraid that they were going to get in trouble for eavesdropping.

"Rickie," she said, "listen. I need you to get online and book four seats on the very next plane to Cleveland today. Use one of the credit cards in my purse. And Bobbie, I need you to throw some clothes in your and Rickie's overnight bags. Can I trust you guys to do that for me and do it fast?"

Both girls nodded. They didn't know what happened but Jaicyn had just given them really important jobs and they were determined not to disappoint.

Once the girls scampered out of the kitchen Jaicyn went back outside to Rayshawn. His tears had stopped but he was staring vacantly at the pool. Jaicyn had a feeling that he was reliving his mother getting killed eleven years ago, especially since he considered King to be the only father he had.

"Baby," Jaicyn whispered, "he's going to be okay. We have to believe that."

"I gotta go to Washington Heights," Rayshawn finally spoke."

"I'm taking care of that. But you have to…." Jaicyn's voice broke off. She was going to say 'snap out of it' but that was insensitive. She really didn't know what to say. If King didn't make it, everything they worked for could come crashing down in an instant.

"I'm alright," Rayshawn assured her and it seemed like he was. He put his hat back on and wiped his face with his shirt.

"Let's go."

****

Four hours after the phone call, Rayshawn and his small family were checked into the Ritz Carlton in downtown Washington Heights and impatiently waiting for Slim to come pick them up. Rayshawn had calmed down tremendously. Now, he was the comforter for his girls as the news of King being shot finally hit them. Plus he realized that the crew was looking to him and he had to handle his business.

Slim didn't think it was a good idea for Rayshawn and Jaicyn to be riding around Washington Heights without any protection so he volunteered to come to the hotel and get them. When Slim called, saying he was in the hotel lobby, Rayshawn interrupted Jaicyn's conversation with her sisters in the bedroom of their hotel suite.

"Slim's here," he announced. "We have to go."

Rayshawn noticed more tears in Rickie and Bobbie's eyes. They were worried about King and wanted to go to the hospital. Jaicyn refused. They didn't need to see King in a hospital bed.

If someone had predicted that when Rayshawn was recruited to work for King, that he, Dayshawn, King, Sandy, Jaicyn, and her sisters would be closer than a family that shared the same blood Rayshawn wouldn't have believed it. He completely understood why Rickie and Bobbie were distraught. He also knew that Jaicyn didn't have the words to comfort

48

them because there were no words. No one had any real information as to what had happened except King and Blaque and both of them were unconscious.

Jaicyn kissed her sisters on their foreheads and stood up.

"We'll be back. I'll call you when I know something."

She ruffled Bobbie's ponytail. "It's going to be okay Muffin."

Rayshawn remembered hearing those same words when he was eleven. His mother's best friend had hugged him and Dayshawn as they loaded Shani's bleeding body into an ambulance and told them the same thing.

The twins had been asleep when Jared came home from a party. Shani was sitting at the dining room table making jewelry. The beaded necklaces and ornate bracelets had become a hobby of hers, a hobby that she only got to do after the boys were asleep and her husband wasn't home demanding all of her attention.

Jared had spent the evening drinking and partying with his brothers and sisters. No knew what happened that prompted him to come home and start the fight with his wife. The argument was loud and Jared had slapped Shani. The twins had woke up when they heard Shani yelling at her husband. Rayshawn had wanted to help her but Dayshawn held him back. Their parents had been arguing more than usual over the past few months but the fights never turned violent.

When they heard the loud slap followed by Shani's screams, Dayshawn snuck out of the bedroom and used the cordless phone to call 911. The cops arrived at the same time Jared fired two shots from his revolver into his wife's chest.

Shani died on the way to the hospital and everything was not okay.

When Rayshawn and Jaicyn got in Slim's car, no one spoke a word even though they hadn't seen each other in months. Slim's leg twitched like it always did when he was upset. He was on edge. Rayshawn had hoped that the flight from Los Angeles would have taken some of Slim's edge off but it hadn't. He hoped the man was smart enough not to go shoot up all of Washington Heights.

When Slim pulled his rental into the Emergency Room lot, Sandy was waiting for them with her son Andre Carter Jr.; AJ for short. Sandy looked terrible. At seven months pregnant with her second child and her husband in a hospital bed, no one expected her usual fashion show.

When she saw Rayshawn and Jaicyn she burst out in tears and wrapped her arms around them in a tightly. Jaicyn held onto Sandy the longest and tightest. She knew what Sandy was going through. The woman was actually living Jaicyn's worst nightmare. All Jaicyn could do was hold her hand and make sure she had a strong shoulder to cry on.

Rayshawn and Slim walked up to King's room in the ICU. For security purposes, Sandy had insisted that Blaque and King be in the same room. Corey, Marcus, Little Man, and Johnny were keeping watch outside the door. No one knew who had pulled the trigger but they weren't taking any chances that someone would try to finish the job.

Their hard edged expressions softened a little when Slim rounded the corner with Rayshawn by his side. Corey and the others were worried that Rayshawn wasn't going to come back to Washington Heights. Seeing him almost made the crew happy. Tonight, with King shot and Rayshawn in town, they'd earn their pay for real.

"What's the word?" Rayshawn asked.

"Blaque's gon be alright," Corey answered. "He caught one in the thigh and in the shoulder."

"And King?" Rayshawn wanted to know.

Corey shook his head from side to side. "He's all fucked up. Two in the chest, close to his heart. They say it's touch and go. He's in a coma."

"I'm goin' in," Rayshawn said, looking at the closed door. "Then we'll talk."

Rayshawn walked into the dim and sterile room. The monitors keeping tabs on King's vital signs hummed and beeped. A young nurse was checking Blaque's bandages. She smiled when she saw Rayshawn.

"Are you his son?" she asked, looking towards King.

"Yeah," Rayshawn choked out. He never imagined that he'd be staring at King lying in a hospital bed in a coma. He wasn't handling it well.

The young nurse smiled soothingly.

"I'm Tracy," she introduced herself. "I'm your dad's nurse."

"Is he gonna make it?" Rayshawn hesitated to ask but he had to know. It didn't look like King would make it, with all those tubes and machines he was hooked up too. Rayshawn had only seen ventilators in movies and the person it was attached to never made it.

Tracy looked down at King and then at Rayshawn.

"He's fighting," she answered slowly. "You should talk to his doctors and surgeon. I'll get them for you."

When Tracy left the room, Rayshawn walked over to King's bed and sat down in the chair. He stared at King. When the boss got hit, shit had to get handled and fast. King had millions of dollars at stake plus a wife and two kids. His empire was strong. As long as Rayshawn was alive, it would remain that way.

"King," Rayshawn said in a low voice, "I'm here. You don't have to worry about nothing. I got you man."

Rayshawn stared at King, hoping to see some type of acknowledgement but King didn't move. Rayshawn got up and walked over to Blaque's bed. His arm was in a cast. So was his leg. Other than that he looked normal. He opened his eyes when he felt Rayshawn staring at him.

"What's up," Blaque said hoarsely. "It's good to see you man."

"Not like this," Rayshawn answered.

"It's all good," Blaque said. "I trust that you got this taken care of."

"Yeah," Rayshawn replied. "I'm going to take care of everything."

"I believe you. Is King gonna live?" Blaque asked but Rayshawn shrugged.

"Get some rest, man," he said. "I'll be back."

Rayshawn walked out of the room with his hands tucked deep into his jeans pockets. Sandy and Jaicyn had joined the crew. Sandy was still holding Jaicyn's hand when Rayshawn spoke to her.

"What did the doctor say?"

"One of the bullets went through his lung," Sandy cried. "They had to put him in a coma so he wouldn't have to breathe on his own. They say we just have to wait and pray."

Rayshawn shut his eyes for a second. This was worse than his mom. He didn't want to wait and see if King was going to make it. Waiting would kill him.

Get it together, he scolded himself and opened his eyes.

"Call K-ci and Sonny and have them meet us at the Park," he ordered Little Man. "The rest of y'all, strap up and head over there too."

In this situation, Oak Park projects was the safest place for anyone in King's crew. Plus it was the best place to get information. When something as serious as the kingpin getting shot happened, the streets would be hot with gossip. And Rayshawn needed to know who had done this.

The crew fell in line like soldiers and started to walk away. Sandy dropped Jaicyn's hand and grabbed Rayshawn's arm.

"All of you can't go! You can't leave him here without any protection, Rayshawn!"

Slim and Rayshawn looked at Jaicyn.

"Give me a piece," she said. "Me and Johnny will hang back."

Slim handed Jaicyn a small handgun that she skillfully tucked under her sweater.

"You know what to do," he said. Jaicyn nodded.

Next to Blaque and Slim, none of the guys could think of anyone who'd do a better job of looking out for King than Jaicyn. If anyone came near King's door that wasn't wearing scrubs and hospital identification she would blow their head off in the middle of the ICU and not think twice.

Rayshawn gave Sandy a hug and Jaicyn a quick kiss.

"I'll be back later, I promise."

"It's all good, baby," Jaicyn assured him. "Handle your business."

CHAPTER 6

Rayshawn stood in the kitchen in the 'main house', the apartment that served as headquarters for the Little Man and the Oak Park dealers. Seated at the table were Corey, Marcus, Slim, Johnny, and Little Man. K-ci and Sonny had found chairs and pulled them into the kitchen. Rayshawn fully expected t the men gathered in front of him to know why they were there and have some answers for him.

"You know why you're here," Rayshawn started, "so let's get to it. What the fuck happened?"

"People are sayin' some west side niggas shot up the dealership," Corey spoke up.

"That's not good enough! What people? What niggas?" Rayshawn yelled. "The west side is full of niggas! I need more than that!"

"They say it might have been Ramel and his crew," Corey added.

Rayshawn rolled his eyes to the ceiling. He couldn't believe that his crew was giving him 'maybe' and 'might haves' when he wanted definite answers.

"Who the fuck are 'they'?" Rayshawn yelled.

Little Man grimaced at the ferocity in Rayshawn's voice. Rayshawn's poor anger management hadn't gotten any better over the years. Little Man knew that the halfhearted effort that the crew had made to find King's shooters was enough to make Rayshawn completely lose it.

It was too soon to know anything though. News didn't travel as fast as it once did in Washington Heights. People on the streets were speculating, but without knowing if King was going to live or die, whoever did the shooting was keeping quiet. It could be days or even weeks before they found out anything concrete.

Little Man knew that if he didn't find out something soon, Rayshawn would be the first to lose his composure, followed by Slim. He had tried to get a handle on the situation before Rayshawn got to Washington Heights but didn't have any luck. If somebody didn't find out something soon, Rayshawn and Slim were likely to hit the streets of Washington Heights and shoot anyone they thought had information.

"It's just what people in the hood are guessing," Little Man tried to clarify. "No one really knows anything yet, Rayshawn. But we're on it. You just got to relax and give us a few days. We'll find them."

Rayshawn looked at the supposed leaders of King's crew and took a deep breath. He tried to calm himself before he said something that he really didn't mean.

"All of you are slackin' off and there's no excuse for that shit," Rayshawn said. "This is the south side. I don't care how long I've been gone, but I know that niggas from the south side don't let people get away with shit like this. Every single one of us in this room would either be broke or dead if it wasn't for King and Blaque. They're laying up in hospital beds and all you can say is we'll get them. Fuck that!"

He looked around the room at all seven guys. All were looking right back at him. This was a moment that they'd been waiting for; the moment that Rayshawn had been groomed for. King had spent years teaching him how to control the streets. They were glad to see him acting like the boss, finally.

"Last time I checked we run this damn city. We make people talk. I shouldn't have to tell you that. We need to be on the west side hunting those niggas down, making people talk. I don't care what it takes. If you're going to act like a girl and whine about drug wars and gun fights, go home. But remember, there are consequences for not stepping up."

Rayshawn stopped talking long enough to catch the fear on K-ci and Sonny's faces. They had always been the weakest in King's crew. Hell, Sonny was even scared of Jaicyn. That's why she was able to take corners away from him when she was running the Park. Rayshawn's speech had little effect on the two cowards. Everybody stayed in their seats though.

"I'm not bullshittin'," Rayshawn yelled. "Get the fuck out of here and do something! Bring me a name and hurry the fuck up!"

He walked out of the kitchen and sat down on a couch. The apartment looked exactly as he and Jaicyn had left it three years ago. It still felt like *his* place...comfortable. He reached for the half finished blunt in an ashtray and lit it.

Rayshawn hadn't smoked weed since he left Washington' Heights. The smoke burned his lungs as he inhaled. He choked back a cough and held the smoke in his lungs. The first toke had him feeling light headed but it passed.

Slim sat down across from Rayshawn when the others left the apartment. He knew his role without anyone saying anything. Rayshawn was home and until he was back on a plane to Atlanta, Slim would be right there watching his back. Rayshawn passed him the blunt.

"How are things in Atlanta?"

"It's all good," Rayshawn lied. He didn't want to get in to the trouble he was having finding D-train. "Heard you're doin' big things in Cali."

"Yeah," Slim agreed, "you could say that. Got my real estate license like Jay-Jay. Gotta turn that good drug money into good legit money."

"Same here," Rayshawn replied. "King taught us that quick."

"Yeah, he taught us a lot. He turned some young hood niggas into real businessmen." Slim laughed and toked his weed.

"He better make it." The worry in Slim's voice caused Rayshawn to look up at him. But he didn't say anything.

"Look, man," Slim said, "I know you're buggin' out. I feel you, bro. King's like my father too. I've been around that man since I was ten years old. I don't have no daddy. He's the only father I know. You don't have to pretend this shit isn't killing you. Not around me."

Rayshawn stared vacantly across the room at the wall then at Slim. His eyes were watering and when Slim blinked, a single tear slid down his cheek.

"He saw something special in you, kid," Slim said. "I remember him saying that all the time."

"He gave me a chance," Rayshawn mumbled. "I probably would've ended up selling dope anyway, but he taught me the right way to do it. He taught me what a real family is supposed to be."

"Same here. But the nigga ain't dead yet, so let's stop talking about him like he is. Hand me that box of Dutches."

Rayshawn passed the box of cigars and waited while Slim rolled them both another blunt. As they smoked Rayshawn thought about everything he left in Washington Heights. Namely his family. Not his flesh and blood family. They still didn't give a shit about him, but the dealers that he spent the majority of his time with.

King had changed Rayshawn's life. He had taken a kid who felt no one cared about him and showed him that life didn't stop just because your real family was fucked up. He showed the twins what it was like to have a real family, people around them that genuinely cared about their well being.

King took two teenage boys under his wing and became a father to them, whether he meant to or not. He did what Jared and Ike Moore had failed to do; taught those boys how to become men. And now that man was in the hospital, weakened by two bullets to the chest and all Rayshawn wanted to do was kill someone.

When his blunt was nothing more than a quarter inch of brown cigar Little Man tossed Rayshawn a Dutch Master and a dime bag. No words were spoken, just blunt after blunt was smoked by the top men in the crew. Rayshawn just wanted to lose himself in the haze of the good Columbian weed. He'd deal with the bullshit later.

****

"Jay-Jay?" croaked the voice in the bed across from King.

Jaicyn was dozing in the chair next to King's bed when she head Blaque say her name. She got up and walked over to his bed.

"What's up?" she greeted him sleepily.

"What time is it?"

Jaicyn looked at her watch. "12:30. Why? You got someplace to be?"

"No," Blaque said and managed a small smile. "Who's here?"

"It's just me right. now"

Jaicyn had sent Sandy and AJ home. Johnny went home to shower and was coming right back. It had been two days but Jaicyn hadn't left King or Blaque's side at all.

"How's King? He alive?"

Jaicyn nodded. Since she'd gotten to the hospital, Blaque had the one moment with Rayshawn where he was conscious. But then he started to have an allergic reaction to the medication they gave him and he lost consciousness for a minute. He'd been out of it for the most part.

"They say he's going to make it. He woke up once but the doctors don't think he's ready to breathe on his own yet. They're gonna take him off the respirator in a couple of days. How are you feeling?" Jaicyn asked.

"I'll be fine," Blaque answered. "Did they say when I could go home?"

Jaicyn shook her head. She knew that Blaque was anxious to get out of the hospital but she didn't have any answers for him. All she knew was that his shoulder and leg wounds were more serious than he thought.

"They didn't say," she answered and sat in the chair next to Blaque's bed. She watched as he struggled to adjust his bed and pillow with his one good arm.

"I can help you with that," she commented.

Blaque laughed. "I know. I just didn't want to ask."

Jaicyn smiled warmly. It was just like Blaque to not want to show any sign of weakness. Rayshawn was like that too. It bugged the hell out of her.

"Any word from Rayshawn?" Blaque asked.

"No," Jaicyn said with a frustrated sigh. "I've been calling but Rayshawn's got nothing. I don't think they know anything. Do you know who did this?"

"I think so," Blaque said. "But it was dark so I'm not completely sure."

"What happened that night?" Jaicyn asked since it seemed like Blaque was in the mood for talking.

"We were leaving the dealership, about to grab something to eat at Sandy's. It was about nine o'clock so it was dark. I didn't see any cars or nothing," Blaque told her.

He heard a quiet pop. He knew what guns with silencers sounded like. Blaque had been around guns all his life. He told Jaicyn that grabbed his gun. All he and King could do was shoot back even though they couldn't see anybody. They couldn't go back inside because the door was locked. They'd be dead before King could unlock the door. The only thing that they could do was run to the car.

He and King started shooting in the direction they thought the shots were coming from but they kept coming and eventually both of them got hit. King fell when he took the shots in the chest. Blaque caught one in his shoulder trying to cover King. He took another in the leg while he was trying to get King in the car.

"But you don't know who it was?" Jaicyn asked. She felt sick after hearing Blaque's account of the shooting.

"I don't know for sure but the dude laughed when King fell. It sounded like Ramel."

Jaicyn sucked in her breath. Ramel! Just hearing his name sent her reeling.

"Seriously?" Jaicyn managed to ask.

"I wouldn't bet my life on it, but I'm almost sure. It makes sense," Blaque replied. "He's been talking shit about Rayshawn since he got out and he's pissed that all of his good people work for us now. I thought I handled his ass a few weeks ago but that nigga is crazy. He just can't let shit go."

"I know. You think he did this to get back at Rayshawn?"

"That and other reasons," was Blaque's sleepy answer.

Sensing that Blaque was getting tired, Jaicyn stopped asking questions and thought about what she'd just heard. She looked over at King. He looked helpless with all the tubes and machines attached to his body and Jaicyn felt responsible.

If Ramel had done this, it was her fault. King had never had any problems with the Puerto Ricans until she came along. She should have taken care of her problems with Ramel before it escalated to this. Now Rayshawn was in danger again. Ramel would easily find out that they were in town and there was no doubt in her mind that her man was on his hit list.

"What you thinkin'?" Blaque asked when Jaicyn got quiet.

"I have to do something about Ramel. We both know that he's going to try and hit Rayshawn next. That boy is reckless."

Blaque shook his head. Even hurt, he was looking out for Jaicyn, always her protector. He didn't want her out there trying to do anything to Ramel Cruz. Ramel was trying to avenge his uncle's death and his prison sentence. Jaicyn was just as much on his hit list as Rayshawn and King.

"That's the last thing you need to do," Blaque said. "You need to let the others handle it."

"Why? Because I'm a girl?" Jaicyn sneered angrily. "Look at you! Look at King! This is happened because of Ramel's beef with me and I'm going to put an end to this shit once and for all!"

"Calm down," Blaque said calmly, his tone typical of himself. Even being shot up in the hospital didn't rattle Blaque and he wasn't going to sit there and listen to Jaicyn fly off the handle.

"That's the problem with you and Rayshawn. You can't control your emotions and be ready to shoot without consequence. That ain't cool. This has nothing to do with you. Ramel is on some other shit and we have people to take care of him. Let them do their jobs. When has it ever been your job to be muscle?"

Jaicyn stared at the floor, feeling like she was being scolded by her big brother.

"Whatever," she muttered.

"Don't 'whatever' me," Blaque said. "You know I'm right. King has the people in place where he wants and needs them to be. Respect the organization that he put together and do your part. Let Slim, Corey, Marcus, and Rayshawn take care of this."

Jaicyn disagreed but didn't argue. She couldn't convince Blaque that she was right. She had no intention of sitting back twiddling her thumbs and playing babysitter while her arch enemy roamed around Washington Heights gunning for her man.

"What's wrong?" Johnny said, entering the room. Rayshawn and Slim were right behind him and they noticed the angry look on Jaicyn's face as soon as they stepped in the room.

"Nothing," Jaicyn said standing up. "Rayshawn, can I talk to you for a minute?"

Rayshawn was quietly staring at King. He hadn't been back to the hospital since the first day. He still couldn't believe that this was happening. Jaicyn noticed him standing over the bed with his shoulders quivering and went over to him.

"He's going to be okay, Rayshawn. It looks worse than it is," she said soothingly. "Can I talk to you for a sec?"

Rayshawn followed Jaicyn out of the room until she found an empty corridor.

"What's up?" Rayshawn asked. He was eager to talk to King's doctor, not Jaicyn.

"Blaque told me who did this."

"Who?"

"Ramel."

Rayshawn nodded his head slowly. "That's what Slim thinks too."

"We have to take that nigga out, Rayshawn," Jaicyn urged. "Me and you."

Rayshawn laughed. "Me, yeah. You, hell no! You ain't getting caught up in this."

Jaicyn wasn't deterred. She had expected a similar reaction from Rayshawn, but she wasn't going to let anyone stop her from doing what she felt she had to do.

"This is not the time for your male chauvinistic shit," Jaicyn fired back. "This is our problem; yours and mine. Not anyone else's and you know it. I refuse to hang back and watch from the sidelines. I know how Ramel thinks. I've known him since I was eight. He's coming for you next. And if he can get to King, in this city, what makes you think he can't get to you? And I'm not having that."

"No," Rayshawn repeated. "Baby, I appreciate your willingness to help but you're not looking at the bigger picture. I don't want shit to happen to you."

Jaicyn folded her arms across her chest. Her lips were tight and the little vein in her neck that throbbed when she was angry was out of control.

"That's bullshit and you know it. The same shit that can happen to me out there can happen to you. Eight years ago, I was the one in the hospital and I had no choice but to let you take care of Mario. But this is now, and I'm knee deep in this game, right along with you, Blaque, Slim and all the others. You can say no until you're blue in the face but I'm not accepting that."

Jaicyn glared coldly at her man. "Either we do it together or I do it alone, doesn't matter to me. One way or another, Ramel is a dead man. And I guarantee you, Rayshawn; I'll find him before any of y'all do." Jaicyn uncrossed her arms and started to walk away.

"Jaicyn!" Rayshawn called but she kept walking. Rayshawn ran after her, calling her name but she didn't stop until she reached the elevators. Rayshawn caught up with her before the doors opened.

"Don't," she said and pushed his hand off of her shoulder. "Go back in there and get your boys. Ramel will be an afterthought before you can even get the crew together."

Rayshawn could see that Jaicyn was dead set on doing something stupid. He hated this side of her. Her alter ego had taken over. The one who knew how to hustle and loved it. The one who wasn't afraid to get her hands dirty if necessary. This was the side of Jaicyn Jones that everyone claimed was just like him. Still, he wasn't going to let her hit the streets of Washington Heights, gunning for one of the city's craziest residents, alone, even if she was capable of doing so.

"Alright," Rayshawn said, reluctantly giving in. "Let's do this."

CHAPTER 7

Jaicyn drove the borrowed Ford Taurus down LaSalle Avenue in LaLa Land like a woman on a mission. She knew the street like the back of her hand. It was the same street her grandmother used to live on.

Rayshawn sat in the passenger seat, feeling anxious and apprehensive. No one in the crew had a clue of what he and his girlfriend were up to and he didn't like that. But it was Jaicyn's idea to go at Ramel alone and reluctantly he was following her lead. She seemed to know what she was doing.

Rayshawn should have been impressed with Jaicyn. She had connections and contacts all over the city. With only two phone calls she had a car and an appointment to see the biggest gun runner in Washington Heights. It was Rayshawn who felt nervous and out of place once they got there.

Blue was one of the most highly respected men in Washington Heights. In all the years that Rayshawn had worked with King and Blaque, he'd never met Blaque's father. He came from a long list gun sellers and Blaque was his only child. He was happy to help Jaicyn out. Knowing that the Prince and Princess of Washington Heights had returned to take care of the situation that landed his only son in the hospital, Blue was happy to provide them with all of the fire power that they needed.

Now Jaicyn was behind the wheel of the Taurus looking out of the window for any sign of Ramel, anyone in his family, or his crew. All of a sudden she pulled the car over to the curb and stared at a girl in a white shorts and a red bikini top who was walking down the street listening to her iPod. Jaicyn cocked the borrowed nine millimeter sitting on her lap and continued to stare out the window as the girl moved closer to the car.

"What are you doing?" Rayshawn asked.

"That's Marisol, Ramel's sister," Jaicyn answered. "I'll be right back."

Before Rayshawn could stop her, Jaicyn swung open the door and started walking towards the young woman who was just minding her own business. Rayshawn watched as Marisol noticed Jaicyn walking towards her with her gun at her side and took off running.

Jaicyn chased her and with Marisol running in heeled sandals and Jaicyn in her Nikes, it wasn't much of a chase. Jaicyn grabbed the girl by her hair and dragged her, kicking and screaming, to the car. Rayshawn had no idea what Jaicyn had in mind but he opened the back door anyway and Jaicyn threw Marisol in.

"¿Qué haces?" Marisol yelled. – *What are you doing?*

"¿Dónde está Ramel?" Jaicyn questioned – *Where is Ramel?*

Marisol stared at Jaicyn with fiery anger in her eyes.

"Fuck you Jaicyn! No estoy diciendo que la mierda!" – *I'm not telling you shit.*

Jaicyn argued with the girl, firing off Spanish sentences in rapid succession. Rayshawn had no idea what they were saying but it was exciting, especially when Jaicyn got out of the car and dragged Marisol out by her hair. Marisol started kicking and her shoes went flying off, almost hitting Rayshawn in the head. Jaicyn punched the petite girl in the stomach and pulled out her gun when Marisol doubled over in pain.

"Where is your brother?" she asked again, this time in English, while she pointed the gun at Marisol's head.

Jaicyn usually used more tactical and reserved ways of getting information out of people but she was very familiar with the Cruz family. They were an unreasonable clan so she was determined to use their same scare tactics to get information out of Ramel's youngest sister. She'd shoot her in broad daylight in the middle of LaLa Land on the 4th of July if she had to. Eventually, with a bullet in both of her knees and elbows, the girl would talk.

Just when Rayshawn thought that Jaicyn was going to pull the trigger and splatter the young girl's brains all over the car Marisol caught her breath and whispered something to Jaicyn.

"What?" Jaicyn said.

"He's at my mother's house," Marisol cried. "Please don't hurt my mother."

Jaicyn stared at the girl with contempt. She reached out and grabbed the cell phone that was clipped to Marisol's shorts and got in the car.

"Ain't nobody gon do nothing to your mother and if you say shit, I'm coming back for you," she said and pulled off, leaving the girl in the street. Jaicyn felt Rayshawn staring at her.

"What?"

"You're crazy," he answered, shocked by what had just happened. "Everybody said you were and they were right."

Jaicyn rolled her eyes. "Who cares? I get the job done."

It didn't take long for Jaicyn to drive two blocks and pull the car to a stop in front of a bright yellow eyesore of a house.

"What the fuck?" Rayshawn said. "This is Ramel's place?"

Jaicyn laughed. She always hated the house. It was ugly and disgusting. Everyone in the neighborhood hated the house but there was nothing that they could do. Ramel would terrorize the neighborhood if anyone said anything to his mother about painting her house or cleaning up her front yard.

"This is his mother's house. Let's see if he's here."

Using his sister's phone, Jaicyn looked for the number to the house. She stared at the front yard while the phone rang. Ramel's black Monte Carlo was parked in the driveway but that didn't mean anything. His beat up Camaro that he'd never got around to fixing was still parked in the front yard, where it had been for the last fifteen years.

"His mother's car isn't here," Jaicyn stated. Suddenly the phone stopped ringing and Jaicyn heard Ramel's voice on the other end.

"¿Qué?"

Jaicyn hung up the phone.

"He's in there," she told Rayshawn. "So if he's there then Paco and Manny are in there too. How do you want to do this?"

"I got the shotgun," Rayshawn said, "so it'll be easier for me to lead. We'll go in the back door and shoot our way to the front if we have to. Just keep the car running."

"Are you really ready for this?" Rayshawn asked Jaicyn seriously.

He knew what it was like to shoot a man. He knew how seeing a man beg and plead for his life could make you feel. He wasn't sure if Jaicyn could handle it and he didn't need her freezing up instead of pulling the trigger. This wasn't like it was with Mario. He was sure that everyone inside that house had guns. If she did freeze, the likelihood of them getting out of the house alive was slim.

"I'm good," Jaicyn said confidently. "Let's go."

She was the first out of the car and walked with so much determination in her hasty steps that Rayshawn had to jog across the yard to keep up with her. She stopped at the back steps and looked around the backyard. There were a couple of coolers filled with ice and beer and the grill had been cleaned. It looked like the Cruz's were getting ready for a 4th of July party.

The back door opened and Manny, a short stocky man who did everything that Ramel told him to do, stepped out carrying some stereo equipment. He didn't even see Jaicyn or Rayshawn at the bottom of the steps. He was too busy laughing and yelling something to his buddies inside the house. He didn't see who had pulled trigger as his chest exploded from the blast from Rayshawn's shotgun. The stereo Manny was carrying crashed to the ground seconds before his body hit the porch.

Rayshawn ran up the steps, sidestepping the quickly forming pool of blood. Jaicyn followed eager to get inside the house. Another blast from the shotgun ended Paco's life in the hallway, his .45 still in his hand when he fell. Jaicyn felt no remorse over Paco and Manny. She didn't like them either.

Jaicyn peeked into the kitchen but didn't see Ramel. Rayshawn checked the small dining room and started to look around the living room.

"I don't see him," Rayshawn turned towards Jaicyn just as they heard a shot and bullet whizzed past his head.

"He's behind the couch!" Jaicyn yelled and started firing rounds into the couch. Rayshawn followed suit, pumping round after round into the sofa. Ramel kept firing at them. Rayshawn and Jaicyn ducked behind the dining room wall, narrowly avoiding the bullets whizzing past them. Jaicyn's heart pumped ferociously in her chest. So much adrenaline was coursing through her body that she felt lightheaded. When she stopped shooting in order to reload, Ramel jumped out of the open living room window. Rayshawn ran out of the front door with Jaicyn right behind him.

Rayshawn stopped running and fired at Ramel running across the front yard. The shotgun blast hit Ramel in the leg, blowing out his kneecap and he fell. He tried to drag himself to his car. This time Rayshawn and Jaicyn didn't have to run to catch up to him. The young couple walked over to their bleeding enemy and each fired a shot into Ramel's chest. The man who had tried to ruin both of their lives on more than one occasion lay perfectly still, as his blood soaked into the ground. Finally, he was dead.

Jaicyn stared down at Ramel's lifeless body. He tried to make her life miserable every day that she'd known him. He had raped her. He wanted her dead. But she'd gotten to him first because she wasn't stupid and impatient like him.

She poked at his body with the tip of her shoe.

"Fuck you," she whispered. "I hope you rot in hell."

Rayshawn heard the police sirens in the distance and grabbed Jaicyn's hand. They ran to the car, tossed the guns in the backseat and sped off in the opposite direction of the arriving cops. This time Rayshawn drove. He drove straight to the motel room they'd rented. It was a beat up and run down establishment that took cash with no identification required and you could drive straight up to the room, which was exactly what they needed.

They didn't talk while they undressed and stuffed their jeans, t-shirts, underwear, socks, and sneakers into a black garbage bag. One of Rayshawn's favorite TV shows was CSI and even though he knew that

Washington Heights didn't have a police department as dedicated at those guys, he wasn't taking any chances.

Jaicyn and Rayshawn showered together, making sure there was no blood or anything on each other's bodies. In record time they were dressed again, this time looking fresh and fly as usual and back in the Taurus.

"You okay?" Rayshawn asked Jaicyn once they were in the car and headed back to the safety of the south side.

"I'm fine," Jaicyn said. "I don't want to talk about it right now."

Rayshawn thought that she was shaken up by what they'd just done. He expected her to be.

"You'll be alright," he assured her. "Once we get rid of the clothes and the guns we'll be fine."

"I know that," Jaicyn said. "I'm not worried about anything. I just don't want to talk about it right now."

Rayshawn had to respect her wishes. In fact, Rayshawn respected her more than anyone else that he knew. Jaicyn didn't hesitate. She didn't falter and right there, in the car, was the first time she'd showed any type of weakness since she heard about King. She deserved a moment to let it all sink it.

"Take me back to the Ritz," Jaicyn said. "I don't want to go to the Park."

Rayshawn was relieved that Jaicyn didn't want to go to the Park and talk to her friends about what had just went down. It meant that she was more like him than like Slim and the rest of the shooters who like to brag and tell stories about what they did.

The truth was Jaicyn didn't care about retelling the story. She wasn't feeling emotional. She was relieved that it was all over. Ramel was dead and no longer a threat to anyone, especially her. All Jaicyn wanted was the nightmares that she had about the day Ramel raped her to stop. She hoped the fear she felt when Rayshawn was late getting home would subside.

She never told anyone about her nightmares. She didn't want people to tell her it was okay to feel scared. It wasn't okay. She didn't want to be scared. Now it was all over and all she wanted to do was curl up in bed and get the peaceful and restful sleep that she hadn't had in eight years.

CHAPTER 8

Jaicyn pulled the dark comforter up over her chin and groaned at the sunlight. She was too comfortable and too happy about being back in her own bed to get up now. After spending two weeks in Washington Heights sleeping in a hotel, she never wanted to leave her bed.

"Jaicyn, did you make the dinner reservation for tonight?" Rayshawn called from inside the walk-in closet.

"Yes!" she yelled back and kicked the covers off her. She sat up and peered into the closet. "You said dinner at seven at Straits."

She wanted to throw Dayshawn a huge party at a club with all his friends. She wanted to buy out the bar and pop bottles of champagne all night. Dayshawn was graduating from law school! He was the first person they knew who went that far in school! He deserved a party. But neither of the twins wanted a party.

Rayshawn was still reeling from King's shooting and what he and Jaicyn had done in Washington Heights. Dayshawn was happy that he was finished with school but he was anxious to get the day over with so he could go back home and check on King. He hadn't been able to go with his brother when it happened and now that school was finished, all he could focus on was making sure that King knew he cared enough to go back and see him. The twins were getting on a plane the very next day.

Jaicyn walked into the closet and watched Rayshawn just throw his clothes into a suitcase haphazardly until she couldn't watch one more pair of jeans fall on top on his already wrinkled shirts.

"Rayshawn! I pay a lot of money for your clothes. Don't just throw them in there. Fold them!"

"Baby, calm down. They're just pants," Rayshawn said.

He knew that Jaicyn was thinking of more things to complain about. The clothes, the party, him not taking out the trash were all arguments she started since she was forbidden to even mumble another word about the one thing that was really bothering her.

His return to Washington Heights.

Rayshawn didn't give a rat's ass about her attitude. His other family was there, holding things down until he got back. Plus King was still in the hospital. He wouldn't feel right leaving Blaque alone to handle the business while King recovered. Rayshawn was expected to keep things in order, not just by King but by everyone who depended on King in order to feed their families.

"Are you going to stand there and watch me pack?" Rayshawn asked his fiancée, "Or are you going to get dressed? We have to be at the school in a couple of hours."

"I know," Jaicyn rolled her eyes and stepped around her man. She grabbed a dress and a pair of shoes before stomping out of the closet. Rayshawn heard the bathroom door slam and the shower come on.

At first, he tried to understand what Jaicyn's problem was with him going back but he couldn't. Ramel and his boys were dead. The cops weren't looking for their killer anymore. The entire police force was probably glad to have that nuisance out of their way. The mayor should be giving him a parade and a medal for taking care of that problem child. There wasn't a logical reason for Jaicyn to worry.

She just didn't want to be left alone in Atlanta for her own selfish reasons. She'd get over it. She didn't have a choice but to get over it.

Rayshawn walked into the bathroom. Jaicyn was standing at the mirror washing her face while the scalding hot shower filled the bathroom with steam. He stood behind her and wrapped his arms around her waist.

"You mad?"

Jaicyn shook her head and continued to apply the sickly sweet smelling cleanser to her face.

"Why would I be mad? It's not like we didn't just get back from Washington Heights, right? It's not like I don't have some crazy ass fool down here that shot up my car and threatened my life, right?"

Rayshawn kissed Jaicyn's left shoulder softly.

"You're going to be fine," he said between kisses. "You're not scared of D-train."

"So," Jaicyn mumbled. Her resolve was weakening with every kiss. "That's not the point."

She closed her eyes as Rayshawn's large hands caressed her flat stomach and his thick lips kissed her neck.

"What's the point then?"

But Jaicyn had lost her train of thought. Every argument she had, every word of protest left her head at the sound of Rayshawn's sweatpants hitting the floor. He pressed his body against her ass and she moaned.

"You don't play fair."

"I know."

Off came his wifebeater, then his boxers. He unhooked her bra and let it drop to the floor.

"Let's take a shower."

Jaicyn turned around slowly and eyes Rayshawn's thick erection.

"Shower, huh? That's all you want to do?"

Rayshawn smirked. "Nope."

"Too bad," Jaicyn grinned. "We have to be the school in a couple of hours.

****

Rayshawn and Dayshawn stood outside the Cincinnati airport waiting for Raul Valdez to pull his bullet proof, black on black Range Rover to a stop.

"Hola Rayshawn!" the son of the Cesar Valdez yelled at Rayshawn like he was greeting an old friend. "Que pasa?"

"It's all good."

The relationship between the two men had started off rocky. Cesar's sons were close to King but hadn't trusted Rayshawn in the beginning. He didn't trust them either. They were two Columbian hotheads who shot first and never asked questions. The brothers were an integral part of their father's empire. The half million dollars worth of dope that King bought every month was chump change to them.

Over the years, the brothers had tested Rayshawn's integrity, loyalty, and manhood every chance they got. He'd passed every test. By the time he and Jaicyn had moved to Atlanta, they had begun to treat him the same as King.

That's why he had called Raul and set up the meeting with Cesar before he and Dayshawn touched down in Washington Heights. King wasn't able to make decisions yet, nor had he talked to Cesar about Rayshawn's idea before he got shot.

Rayshawn had to make things happen quick. The only logical thing to do was to talk to Cesar himself, but he had to get the man to actually talk to him. The best way to do it was cut his sons a side deal.

Raul and Cortez agreed to twenty percent cut of Rayshawn's profits if their father agreed to supply him. King and Rayshawn would split the other eighty percent, with King getting thirty. Jaicyn wasn't going to be happy when Rayshawn told her that they'd only be keeping half of their money but he had no other choice.

They needed to get off the streets. Street level dealers were getting locked up every day in Atlanta. He didn't like putting himself or his girl at risk like that. If someone in their camp got knocked, he couldn't trust that they would just take the years and not rat him or Jaicyn out. The Atlanta dealers weren't family.

Not like his people in Washington Heights.

When the Range Rover pulled into the Valdez compound, Dayshawn let out a low whistle. Rayshawn grinned. His brother had never been to the estate. Hopefully, he never would have to come back.

Still, the sheer magnificence of the estate couldn't be ignored. The freshly manicured lawn, the sprawling mansion, and ornate decorations made the house look more like a museum in Europe than a house in Ohio that people actually lived in.

"Damn," Dayshawn said, staring ahead at the house. "This is the biggest house I've ever seen. Why isn't King living like this?"

"Because King doesn't supply good Columbian dope to most of North America," Rayshawn replied. "Stay cool," he advised his brother. "Cesar doesn't like it when people act all awestruck and he usually doesn't conduct business in his home. He's doing me a favor."

The four men walked into the house and stopped by the updated marble fountain in the foyer.

"He's upstairs," Raul said to Rayshawn. "You come with us," he told the other twin. "Papa wants to talk to your brother in private."

Dayshawn shot a worried glance at his brother who already headed up the white carpeted staircase.

"It's cool," Rayshawn assured him.

"And don't forget to tell him about our deal," Cortez added. "He won't like you keeping that a secret."

Rayshawn nodded and continued up the stairs to the room where he'd first met Cesar eight years ago.

Cesar was sitting on the couch staring at a chessboard that was on the forty-two inch plasma mounted to the wall. He was playing against the computer.

"The Queen is a bad bitch," Rayshawn commented.

"Always. The Queen is the most powerful piece in the game. What have I always said to you?"

"Protect your Queen at all costs," Rayshawn answered.

"This life we live is like a chess game," Cesar said solemnly while studying the board. "One bad move and it's all over, for you and your Queen. The other player takes over your territory and you're dead. One wrong move, one bad decision and it's all over. Do you understand that?"

"Yes sir," Rayshawn answered respectfully. Cesar wasn't just talking about a chess game anymore. He had something completely different on his mind.

"Andre, you're here about Andre, right?" Cesar asked.

"Something like that," was Rayshawn's reply.

Cesar's eyes tightened and he frowned. "Andre is getting sloppy. He's taking too many chances. What happened to him should have never fucking happened!"

Rayshawn's fists clenched in his pockets. He feared that Cesar would think that fronting him any dope would be too big of a chance.

"All his life," Cesar said, "I've tried to teach that boy to lay low, keep a low profile. This life I've built here didn't happen over night. It's dangerous in America. It's safer to be a drug dealer in Colombia."

Rayshawn grinned. "You've been talking about going back there ever since I've known you."

"I will go back. I won't have a choice."

Cesar turned off the television and stared at Rayshawn.

"You're young," he said. "Young but smart. You're asking for a lot of drugs. What do you plan on doing with all of that dope?"

Rayshawn trusted Cesar. He could tell him his plan without judgment.

"I want out soon," he admitted. "I want a normal life. I want to open a couple of businesses, make sure my brother is set for life, and take my family away from here, from this game."

"I'm only twenty-four," Rayshawn continued. "I don't want to be a forty year old drug dealer. I want to live my life away from all this, on some island somewhere with my wife and kids."

"That's new," Cesar sighed. "You weren't thinking like that a few years ago."

Rayshawn hunched his shoulders and looked down at the floor. "People grow up. Look at King. Look at his wife. I don't ever want

Jaicyn to see me in a hospital bed fighting for my life or locked up behind bars."

Cesar patted Rayshawn on his back. "You're a good kid. Family is important to you. Your woman is important to you. I like that. If my Maria asked me to stop, I'd do it, no questions asked. Family is more important than anything, you hear me."

"Yes sir."

"I'll help you. But," Cesar warned, "do not screw this up. Make a few million and stick to your plan. Don't get greedy and don't get sloppy."

Rayshawn grinned like a kid in a candy store. Cesar was on his side! But that didn't take away from Rayshawn's feeling that Cesar was extremely disappointed in King. Rayshawn hoped that King could make things right with the man who taught him everything.

Rayshawn finally understood that's King's relationship with Cesar went beyond the drugs. They shared the same bond that Rayshawn had with King. Cesar's disappointment would come at a price, a price that Rayshawn didn't want to think about. For now, all he could focus on was making sure that Cesar kept supplying Washington Heights with the dope they were used to and convincing Jaicyn to wire the money to Cesar.

****

Jaicyn tossed the cheap pre-paid phone on the sofa and paced the family room restlessly. She ran her hands through her hair while she replayed the conversation she'd just had with her man through her head.

"Six hundred thousand dollars!" she said out loud. "He can't be serious!"

The amount was all of what she had in one of their accounts and now Rayshawn wanted her to just give it to Cesar!

Sure, he was cutting Rayshawn a great deal and only wanted twenty-five percent upfront, but damn. Six hundred thousand dollars from their stash was going to hurt.

"Baby, we'll make it back in a couple of months. Don't stress over stupid shit," Rayshawn had said before hanging up the phone.

She still didn't like taking orders from him but he was right this time. She handled all of their money, down to the penny. He didn't have access to it, only what she put in their joint account and his separate account. Hell, he didn't even know how much money they actually had. Only one other person had access to the money in case something happened and her father would never give her up.

It was safer that way.

Jaicyn finally sat down and opened up her laptop. She logged into the bank account for Janet Wilson, one of her five aliases and transferred some money to Cesar's numbered account in the Bahamas that she'd memorized. She did this six more times from different accounts until all the money was deposited in his account. She used the untraceable pre-paid phone to call Cortez and let him know the transaction was complete. Then she called Rayshawn.

"Now what do you want me to do?" she snapped when he answered.

"Spread the word. Front five apiece to Rock, Darren, and Lil Joe. The comeback is-"

"Ninety," Jaicyn interrupted. "I know how to multiply, Rayshawn."

He sighed into the phone. He still didn't understand what her problem was. They had to spend money to make money. Giving Cesar six hundred thousand was small compared to what they'd actually make in the long run.

Jaicyn's problem was that she never looked at the big picture. Maybe that's why their relationship and business partnership worked so well. They balanced each other.

Most of the time.

"Don't meet anyone in person, not even Rock," Rayshawn told her. "I'm sending Johnny down there to handle that part. Just until I get back. We're disappearing off the radar, Jaicyn."

"What does that even mean?" she snapped again. Rayshawn was trippin'. They couldn't disappear. They weren't even leaving Atlanta.

"It meant you are not getting involved in any street deals. It means no one talks directly to you about anything. Every deal will be filtered through Johnny. All you have to do is make sure that the product is where it needs to be when it needs to be there, okay?"

"Sure, Rayshawn," Jaicyn replied doubtfully. "How much time do I have before it gets here?"

"Three days. The same set up we've been using. The key to the storage unit will be there tomorrow."

"And when are you coming home?"

On the other end, Rayshawn groaned silently. They had almost two million dollars in dope headed their way and his absence was still Jaicyn's main problem.

"I don't know, babe. King won't be out of the hospital for a couple more weeks. I want to make sure everything is good here before I come back. You can hold it down for a couple of weeks, right?"

"That's not the damn point!" Jaicyn argued.

She wanted him home where she could see him every day and know that he was safe. She didn't want to be alone. She didn't feel completely safe when he wasn't around.

"You'll be fine," Rayshawn assured her. "Start looking for space for your second shop. Take your sisters to Fashion Week or something. Just stay out of trouble. I'll be back before you know it. I love you."

"I love you too. And you be safe, please," she pleaded. "If something happens to you, Rayshawn," Jaicyn stopped talking as a lump formed in her throat.

"Baby, I'm fine," Rayshawn softened his voice. "I will be fine. I don't want to stay here. I'm coming back. Don't worry about anything."

"Okay," Jaicyn whispered. "I just miss you."

"Believe me, I miss you too," Rayshawn said. "And tonight we'll Skype and I'll show you how much."

Jaicyn laid back on the sofa and squeezed her legs tightly together as her body tingled. She smiled. Skype sex!

"You're so nasty," she giggled.

"You love it," Rayshawn replied. "Now get to work and get rid of the phone. It's garbage now."

"Sure thing," Jaicyn answered, slipping back into business mode.

"Love you, babe."

"Love you too," Jaicyn answered and disconnected the call.

"Three hundred fuckin' keys," she whispered. "How the hell am I supposed to get rid of three hundred keys?"

CHAPTER 9

"I'm pissed, that's what's wrong with me, Autumn," Jaicyn yelledd into her cell phone. "King is fine. Rayshawn needs to bring his ass home."

Jaicyn walked behind her sisters through the Target aisles while they shopped for party supplies. Bobbie's birthday was two weeks away and if Rayshawn didn't come home, he was going to miss it.

He said he'd only be in Washington Heights until King got out of the hospital but that two weeks had come and gone. Three months later, Jaicyn was holding down *their* business while Rayshawn held down King's.

"Well, what is he saying?" Autumn asked.

"I'm not speaking to him," Jaicyn answered. "I'm not talking to him until he comes home."

"Well, you better talk to him," Autumn advised. "Washington Heights isn't safe at all. You heard about what happened to Ramel, right?"

"No, what?" Jaicyn expertly feigned innocence.

"He's dead," Autumn sated. "Somebody ran up in his mama's house on the 4th and shot him, Paco, and Manny."

"Damn! That's fucked up!" Jaicyn commented. She made a face at the nosy old woman who was glaring at her for using such foul language.

"I know, right," Autumn continued. "The rest of the family went back to Puerto Rico after the funeral. You know that place isn't safe if the entire Cruz clan can be run out of town."

"Wow," was all Jaicyn said.

"They don't even know who did it," Autumn continued. "My brother said that people thought Slim did it, but it wasn't him. It was probably someone from out of town."

Jaicyn grinned. That was partly true. She was glad that the few people who knew what really happened were keeping their mouths shut. Washington Heights may have had the dumbest police force in the country but it still wasn't a good idea to let too many people know your business. The city loved to gossip.

"Well," Jaicyn replied, "I can't say I'm too broken up about that. You know how I feel about Ramel."

"Yeah, I figured that," Autumn agreed. "But still, if that can happen to Ramel, Rayshawn don't need to be there."

"I agree," Jaicyn said. Her other phone started ringing. "Autumn, I'll call you back later."

Jaicyn hung up with her friend and answered her other phone. Rickie and Bobbie rolled their eyes and continued shopping. Jaicyn's BlackBerry was for business purposes only. Rickie and Bobbie caught hell if they even called that number accidently. They knew that if the other phone rang then their sister would be completely distracted.

"This is Jaicyn," she said into her phone while she fumbled around for her Bluetooth.

"Jaicyn, this is Rick."

Rick Spentz was one of the three accountants Jaicyn hired when she and Rayshawn switched businesses. Rick was an expert at finding ways to clean up dirty money. As a general rule of thumb, Jaicyn didn't usually trust white people but she was confident that Rick could be trusted. As long as he got a substantial cut he was happy.

"What's up Rick? Jaicyn said after she hooked her Bluetooth around her ear.

"I've got bad news," Rick answered. "*Caliente* is being audited."

"I'm being what?" Jaicyn asked. She didn't know what audited meant but it didn't sound good.

Rick explained what auditing was and Jaicyn felt nervous. She knew that between lawyers, accountants, and herself, the money was well protected from even the most thorough IRS auditor. Still, she couldn't help but wonder why this was happening or if she'd made some type of mistake. Rick informed that they had a week before the audit and that his firm would go over every record with a fine tooth comb but she needed to be there too.

When she hung with her accountant Jaicyn gave Rickie her debit card and instructed the girls to finish shopping because she had to make an important call. As soon as she got in her car she called Rayshawn.

"You need to come home," was what she said when he answered.

"Oh, you're talking to me now?" Rayshawn commented.

"Whatever," Jaicyn said. "You need to come home."

"Jay-Jay, we already talked about this," Rayshawn groaned. "I'll be home in a couple of weeks."

"No, seriously, Rayshawn, you need to come home now."

Jaicyn told Rayshawn about her phone call from Rick but Rayshawn didn't seem worried like his fiancée. King got audited all the time. It wasn't anything to be worried about. He assured Jaicyn that she was reading too much into it. Jaicyn wasn't convinced. She had a weird feeling that something bad was about to happen.

****

For three days, Jaicyn's stomach was in knots. Her shoulders felt heavy as the undeniable feeling that something bad was about to happen weighed her down.

As she sat in the bleachers of the high school gym, she watched fifteen girls and three boys practice heel lift pyramids and basket tosses until she couldn't keep her legs from trembling anymore. Jaicyn climbed down out of the bleachers and walked outside. After sitting inside the musky sweat filled gym, she was grateful for the blast of fresh air.

The heavy gymnasium door slammed shut and Jaicyn was alone. She wanted to speak to Rayshawn but she knew that he wouldn't have anything to say that would make her feel better, to make her feel safer. All she needed from him was for him to come home. His presence was the only thing she needed to feel safe again. Since she couldn't talk any sense into Rayshawn, she decided to plead her case with his brother. Maybe Dayshawn could talk some sense into his twin.

"What's up Jay-Jay?" Dayshawn's voice was tired.

Fresh out of law school, he spent his days endlessly studying for the Georgia Bar Exam. In order to secure his position at the law firm where he was interning, he had to pass the exam on the first time. Jaicyn's phone call was a much needed distraction.

"Can you please talk to your brother and get him to come home?" Jaicyn asked, getting straight to the point of her interruption. Her straight talk wasn't unusual. She never saw the need in beating around the bush and wasting precious time when she had something to say.

"Why? What's the problem? Do you need something?"

"I need him," Jaicyn stated. "Something feels wrong, Dayshawn. I have this horrible feeling that something is going to happen to him and I can't shake it."

"I'll talk to him," Dayshawn replied. "I can't make you any promises though."

"I'll take what I can get," Jaicyn sighed. "Just talk to him."

"Alright, I'll call you tomorrow then."

Jaicyn hung up the phone and went back inside the gym until cheerleading practice was over.

****

Jaicyn heard the doorbell ring and looked at the time on her phone. It was almost ten o'clock at night and she wasn't expecting anyone.

"Jay-Jay, you got company," Rickie announced as she led Johnny into Jaicyn's office.

Jaicyn rolled her eyes at Rickie's butchering of the English language. She didn't want her sisters taking like the ghetto girls in their school, another reason she wanted them in private school. Rickie and Bobbie were going to be different than her. They were going to have a different life.

They were going to dress differently, talk differently, and live differently than she did when she was their age. They'd never have to worry about where their next meal was coming from or if they would have warm clothes for the winter.

Never again.

Jaicyn would sell drugs for the rest of her life to make sure of that.

"It's Jay-Jay, you have company," Jaicyn corrected her sister. "Now get out of here and wash the dishes. We don't have a maid."

Johnny grinned as Rickie muttered something along the lines of "I'm not the maid either" and stomped out of the room. He sat down on the other end of the cream leather sectional in Jaicyn's office.

"Why are you here?" Jaicyn asked. It was unusual for Johnny to come over to her house without calling. Rayshawn's direct order when he sent Johnny to Atlanta was that he and Jaicyn never talk business in his house and this didn't look like a social call.

Of course she and Johnny still hung out. Johnny being in Atlanta felt like home. Occasionally, Jaicyn missed Washington Heights but now that King was doing better, she didn't feel the need to go back...ever.

"Did we have plans?"

Johnny shook his head. "No, but I think you need to know that Rock's stash house got raided early this morning. They locked up two dudes and APD is looking for him. You know that nigga ain't gonna do no years for me and you."

Jaicyn rubbed her temples and moaned. She had a suspicion that something like this would happen. She didn't have to be out there hustling to know that Rock was living recklessly. He was finally making the type of money that he thought he deserved and acted like he was big shit in Atlanta. Obviously he had never heard of keeping a low profile.

He drove a fifty thousand dollar car and kept it parked in the poorest neighborhood in the city. He went to clubs and bought out the bar. He wasted money by "making it rain" on strippers. He had no real source of income. He wasn't smart enough to have a legit job, if only on paper. He had no connections to get shit like that done. Atlanta police weren't nearly as stupid as Washington Heights' police so of course they noticed his dumb ass. It was only a matter of time before they did something about it.

"I knew that nigga was going to fuck it up for everybody," Jaicyn grunted.

She dug around in her purse until she found the new pre-paid phone she used to talk to Rayshawn. Although she wasn't fond of having to buy a new phone every couple of days, the cheap Trac-fones were virtually untraceable. Better to spend fifty bucks a week than spend a lifetime in jail.

"What's good?" Rayshawn said when he answered.

"Nothing," Jaicyn said and relayed Johnny's story.

"And don't say we're trippin', Rayshawn. This isn't good and you know it."

"I agree, but if you and Johnny have been doing things like I said, Rock shouldn't be even know where his dope is coming from. All he should know is that you're out and Johnny is his new contact. No real names either."

"We're sticking to the plan," Jaicyn huffed.

"Good. Then all we need is to send Johnny home before Rock gets locked up. He'll be fine."

"That's all?" Jaicyn questioned. "Just send Johnny home and forget about it? That's all you got?"

"That's all that needs to be done," Rayshawn insisted. "But if you want, I'll get my brother to ask around and see if there's any heat on us."

"Dayshawn? He's not even a lawyer yet!" Jaicyn shouted. "We pay real lawyers for shit like this!"

"Can't bring the lawyers in right now," Rayshawn tried to explain as quickly as possible for Jaicyn could start yelling louder. "A bunch of lawyers asking questions raises suspicions."

As much as Jaicyn disagreed with her man's logic, she was happy that he said "asking" instead of "axe-in". The boy was a slow learner.

"Alright," Jaicyn replied doubtfully.   She didn't agree with Rayshawn's logic but she didn't know what else to do.

"You sound nervous," Rayshawn said when Jaicyn took a big sigh into the phone. "Don't be. It's gonna be alright."

"Well, I wouldn't be so nervous if I wasn't dealing with this bullshit by myself."

Rayshawn heard the fear in Jaicyn's voice and made a decision. It wasn't the right time to leave Washington Heights. King was doing much better but he was still vulnerable. There were too many other dealers who wanted the south side and Rayshawn wasn't sure how strong King's people actually were.

But he had to go. The crew could take care of themselves. He owed it to Jaicyn to take care of her.

****

"Girls!" Jaicyn called down into the basement where a bunch of twelve year old girls were coming off their sugar high. Cake, ice cream, pop, candy, and any other junk food they could stuff their faces with were spread all over the basement.

Bobbie's Pajama Jammy Jam was off the hook. Jaicyn had managed to pull the party together despite the stress she was under and Bobbie was completely happy.

"Y'all need to hit the showers and put on clean pajamas on while Rickie cleans up down there!"

Cleaning up after Bobbie and her messy friends was Rickie's punishment for skipping cheerleading practice to hang out at Lenox Mall.

If she had asked, Jaicyn probably would have let her go. Instead, she was being punished.

The patio door slip open and the twins came back into the house. They'd chosen to miss the chaos of the teen birthday party and had sat outside talking for the last couple of hours.

"What have you two been doing this whole time?" Jaicyn sniffed the air around the young men to see if they'd been smoking without her. They hadn't.

"Sit down," Rayshawn ordered. "We need to talk."

The somberness in his voice made Jaicyn sit down on one of the counter barstools immediately. She looked back and forth between the twins, waiting for one of them to speak. It didn't matter which one.

"I've got some information," Dayshawn told Jaicyn.

Jaicyn eyed Dayshawn. Before she met them the only way she could tell them apart was by the way that they dressed. Even now, as adults, their clothes were still the best way to tell them apart.

Dayshawn was more distinguished than his brother. He even had on a sleek pair of Louis Vuitton eyeglasses despite having perfect vision.

"Okay," Jaicyn said, "talk."

"There is an investigation going on," Dayshawn sadly said. From the look on his face, he'd already broke the news to his brother. "The FEDS want Cesar, but they'll never get him. That means they'll go after anyone associated with him, especially King and anyone connected to King."

Dayshawn had a hard time looking his brother in the face after telling him he might go to prison for a very long time. The bond the twins had was stronger than the normal "twin thing". They depended on each other. Their family had turned their collective back on them a long time ago. The truth was, they only had each other.

"Who's conducting this investigation?" Jaicyn asked.

"It's a combination of different agencies but it's being spearheaded by the FBI," Dayshawn answered.

As soon as Rayshawn told him about the heat coming down on the Atlanta dealers, Dayshawn jumped to action. There was a girl that he went to law school with that worked for the GBI. She had him in her sights for three years. He called Monique and she called her father, Special Agent Lamont Fuller with the FBI.

All it took was dinner and a six pack to loosen the tongue of Special Agent Fuller. He was eager to impress Dayshawn, who had the potential to be an excellent husband for the agent's scatterbrained daughter. Dayshawn told him he was studying RICO laws for the bar. Agent Fuller didn't hesitate to give Dayshawn some real life examples of active investigations, all classified of course.

"What do we do?" Jaicyn asked. "We can't just sit here and wait for the FEDS to run up in our house."

"We have to see what King wants to do," was Rayshawn's answer.

"King?" Jaicyn yelled. "Why do we need to wait for him to tell us what to do? His ass is going to jail too!"

Rayshawn shot Jaicyn stern warning glare but she ignored it.

"All I'm saying is that they're not going to arrest King before they arrest you. They'll try to use you to get at him.

"She's right," Dayshawn agreed. "You're more at risk than King is. King has some of the best lawyers and cops on his payroll. Do you really think that he doesn't know what's going on? He's probably already planning on leaving the country. He's just waiting to see which one of you gets knocked first."

Rayshawn shook his head. "King wouldn't do that to me. He wouldn't put me out there like that."

"That's what you think," Jaicyn argued. "He'll look out for his own family first. We have to look out for us."

"We are family," Rayshawn growled. He was upset that Dayshawn and Jaicyn didn't have any faith in King after all he'd done for them. "Y'all actin' like King ain't never did shit for us!"

Jaicyn rolled her eyes. "I'm not saying that. But when it comes down to the nitty gritty of it all, I'm looking out for what's mine, and I'm not waiting on King to tell me shit."

Dayshawn gave Rayshawn a questioning glance. Rayshawn was torn. Jaicyn didn't understand why, but Dayshawn saw it. Her relationship with King was different than the twins'. Dayshawn didn't want anything to happen to King but he didn't want to see his brother locked up either.

Rayshawn caught Dayshawn's eye. "What are you thinkin'?"

"You do need to talk to King and see what he knows. But ultimately, I don't think you should be ready to take a fall for him."

Jaicyn looked back and forth between the twins angrily.

"Both of y'all are trippin'. I say we pack our shit and get the hell out of here. I know for a fact that's what King and Sandy are going to do as soon as your ass gets arrested, Rayshawn. If we stay here we're going to lose every fucking thing! And you'll be in prison."

Rayshawn ignored Jaicyn's outburst. She was paranoid and looking for a reason to move to Puerto Rico.

"How much time do we have?" Rayshawn asked his brother.

"From what I could get out of Agent Fuller, they just started the investigation. They're hoping some of these Atlanta dealers will talk. But if you've been doing what you say you've been doing, they don't really know anything. It's going to take six months to a year for them to put together a solid case," Dayshawn answered.

Rayshawn was satisfied with that answer. In his world, six months was a long time. He could stack a lot of money and make serious moves in six months. He could set Jaicyn and the girls up in Puerto Rico before he got arrested with six months to prepare. The first thing he had to do was talk to his real lawyers and figure out the best plan of action.

"This sitting around waiting for bad shit to happen doesn't work for me," Jaicyn blurted out. "I don't care about the relationship you have with King. I don't care that you act like he's your father. When the shit hits the fan, Rayshawn, he's going to be just the man that you sell drugs for and he's going to expect you to take the fall for him."

"No he's not," Rayshawn started to say but he was interrupted.

"That shit better not happen!" Jaicyn continued to yell, "Is your family not as important as King's? Is your life not worth as much as his?"

Jaicyn had a point, but Rayshawn couldn't believe that, at the first sign of trouble, she was turning her back on the man who made her. He was pissed that she was acting so ungrateful.

"You've been in this game long enough to know that I ain't snitching on anybody, especially King!" Rayshawn hollered at her. "You don't have to understand why I do what I do. Just accept it. You need to just chill the hell out and let me handle this."

Jaicyn stood up. The barstool crashed to the floor.

Panic mixed with outrage darkened her face. Tears flooded her eyes as she wrung her hands together.

"You're crazy," she half whispered. "We," she pointed to herself and Rayshawn," we built this shit down here with no help from King. You and

I did this, yet we still give him thirty percent of our money because of what you think he did for us."

Jaicyn took a deep breath trying to calm her nerves and say the right thing. She had to make Rayshawn see that he was not using the good sense God gave him. She touched his leg and pleaded with her eyes.

"We're supposed to be in this together. I've been down for you just as long as King has. I'm the one that shares your bed, your home," she paused, "your life. And you want to turn your back on that for him? Are you serious?"

"Jay-Jay," Rayshawn adverted his eyes from her angry glare. "You know the game."

"Fuck the game!" she yelled, completely losing her cool. "Fuck King and all the rest of those niggas in Washington Heights! If you get arrested and take the fall for any of them, Rayshawn…"

"Jay-Jay, calm down!" Dayshawn put his hand on her shoulder. She was trembling from head to toe when she stepped away from his touch.

"No, I won't calm down!" She glared at Rayshawn who still wouldn't meet her eyes.

"If you do that, Rayshawn, if you choose to abandon us, I'm done. As much as I love you, I will take my sisters so far away from here you'll never find me. You and King can sit in prison together because obviously this," Jaicyn slid her engagement ring off of her finger and held it up, "doesn't mean shit!"

Jaicyn threw the five carat diamond ring at her fiancé and walked out of the kitchen. Rayshawn heard her stomp up the stairs to their bedroom and slam the door. This time he wasn't worried about Jaicyn's temper tantrum. He picked up the ring that had hit him in the chest and bounced to the floor.

"She'll be alright," he said to reassure his brother and most importantly himself. "She ain't goin' nowhere."

Then he laughed. "And she ain't getting this ring back either."

Dayshawn looked doubtful. He'd never seen Jaicyn so upset over anything, but he was more concerned about his brother. He could see the fear in his eyes. He knew that Rayshawn was scared about the possibility of going to prison and everything that Jaicyn had yelled at him could be true.

Rayshawn stepped back outside to the bar and poured himself a shot of Hennessy, straight with no ice. Dayshawn followed him out back.

"You want one?" Rayshawn offered his brother.

"Nah, but I'll take a beer."

Rayshawn poured another shot and grabbed two beers from the small fridge behind the bar. He sat down on a chaise and stared at the stars reflecting off the water in the uncovered pool.

"Want to talk about what just happened?" Dayshawn asked.

"Not really," Rayshawn answered. "Just let me think for a minute."

Dayshawn sipped his beer and sat next to his brother.

After a couple of beers the twins decided that they needed something stronger and popped open another bottle of Hennessy. An hour passed and they didn't talk about anything. All Rayshawn could think about was his next move and what to do about Jaicyn.

A lot had changed since they were sixteen. They were about to get married. The problems they had when they were teenagers didn't even compare to what they were facing now. But Rayshawn was more confident than anyone else that everything would be okay.

"You know," Rayshawn finally spoke up. "I've been preparing for something like this. You don't get in the game at fifteen and not prepare for jail. The girls will be alright."

"You can't prepare for a Federal investigation, bro. I told you. This shit is serious."

"I know," Rayshawn said. "But I've kept my shit nice and neat. Always going behind Jaicyn's messy ass and cleaning shit up. The money is well hidden. They might have a little somethin' from Washington Heights but this Atlanta shit was done right." He turned to his brother.

"I promise you, bro. If it comes down to it, I ain't snitchin' and I'll be out in a year. Max."

CHAPTER 10

Rayshawn stood over the bed staring down at his napping fiancée. Jaicyn had just started speaking to him two days ago. The girl could hold a grudge better than anyone he knew. How anyone could live in the same house and sleep in the same bed with someone and not speak to them was weird. But Jaicyn did it. For three long silent months she didn't utter even a single "Hello" to her man.

At least she hadn't left. And she started wearing her ring again.

While Jaicyn fumed, Rayshawn started planning for the day he got locked up. Most of their money was safe. Jaicyn had moved what she could without drawing too much suspicion into numbered Swiss and Caribbean accounts. Despite her anger, she put enough in Dayshawn's account to pay for legal expenses.

He was worried about Jaicyn, even though she wasn't worried about herself. She was right when she said they were in this together. Rayshawn had allowed her work side by side with him. If the police wanted him; they would easily take her too. He couldn't let that happen. His job was to protect her. He wouldn't let her go to jail. She wouldn't last five minutes in jail. He'd spend the rest of his life locked up if that's what it took to keep her free.

He told her that. It wasn't about King anymore. She was the only one who mattered. That's when she started speaking to him again.

"Jaicyn, Autumn's here," he spoke loud enough to wake her. "You know we're the host of this little shindig."

"Which is why I needed a nap," Jaicyn yawned. "How do you expect me to be the life of the party after keeping me up all night?"

Rayshawn laughed. "You kept asking for it. I just do what I'm told."

Jaicyn burst out laughing and threw a small pillow at him. "Yeah right. Go get my friend, you perv. I gotta get dressed."

"How long it is going to take for you to throw on a bathing suit?"

"As long as it takes," Jaicyn replied sarcastically. "Now go!"

A few minutes later, Autumn walked into the bedroom dragging her suitcase behind her.

"Ew!" Jaicyn wrinkled her nose at her friend's disheveled appearance, especially her jean shorts and flip-flops.

"Did you come straight from the airport? Dayshawn didn't even take you home to shower?"

"We'll talk about him later," Autumn promised. "I'll hop in the shower real quick. Look in my bag and check out the bathing suits I brought."

"There better be at least one bikini in there!" Jaicyn yelled after her best friend. "I'm tired of seeing you in one pieces."

She unzipped the suitcase and pulled out a Macy's bag and grinned. Even though her best friend had plenty of fashion sense and money to spare, Autumn still shopped on a budget. At least she had splurged and bought more than one bikini. Thankfully Autumn had moved on from her all black phase. The bag was full of bright colored bikini tops and bottoms.

"Which one?" Autumn asked when she came back into the bedroom wrapped in a towel.

Jaicyn pulled a pink two-piece from the shopping bag and held it up for Autumn.

"This is the one," Jaicyn said. "I like the top. I bet it makes you look like you're not a member of the Itty Bitty Titty Committee."

Autumn burst out laughing. "Girl, they revoked my membership in college!"

"I don't see why," Jaicyn teased her friend. "Ain't nobody checkin' for those double A's that you have."

"Whatever," Autumn said, still laughing. "Not everyone can have those big old triple D jugs you are carrying around. How's your back?"

"My back is fine and I don't have triple Ds," Jaicyn giggled. "And don't be a hater," Jaicyn advised. "It's not becoming for a child psychologist."

Jaicyn looked out of the balcony door, down at the pool. The party was just getting started; however there weren't a lot of girls there. Most of the guys were Dayshawn's frat brothers since the party was to celebrate him passing the bar. A few of them had brought their girlfriends but most left their girls at home, hoping that Jaicyn would invite some of her single friends.

"There's a ton of guys down there," Jaicyn commented. "But you only got eyes for Dayshawn, huh?"

"I've told you a hundred times, Dayshawn and I are not exclusive. I can talk to whoever I want. But it would be very disrespectful to be flirting with any of these guys. They're his friends and frat brothers," Autumn replied.

Jaicyn smiled and slipped on her bathrobe. "I'm going to shower. Don't go down there without me."

When Jaicyn came back into the room ten minutes later, Autumn had changed into her suit and was staring at the size eight white bikini Jaicyn had laid on the bed.

"Since when did you start wearing an eight? Are you gaining weight?"

Jaicyn frowned at her friend. Only Autumn could get away with a question like that. Jaicyn was bone thin in junior high school. Even when she started getting boobs and hips, she was a four or six through high school. She was not happy with being an eight.

"Shut up. I'm joining a gym next week. I'll lose this weight in a month."

Autumn picked up the bathing suit and laughed when she read the label. "Baby Phat? Suits you."

"I'm gonna kick your ass," Jaicyn laughed and snatched the suit. "Here I am, throwing a nice barbeque for your man and you make fun of my weight. Some friend you are."

"Hey, if I can't tell you that you have a little too much junk in your trunk, who can?"

"Whatever. My junk is fine. Look at you!"

Autumn's body was bangin' in her pink bathing suit. Jaicyn was a little jealous.

"I guess your man will love that," Jaicyn commented. "He always did like them thick."

"Whatever, Jaicyn," Autumn smiled. "He needs to pay attention to me. He hasn't been."

"In that bathing suit, he's not going to be looking at anyone else. He better get together. You're a catch. He better recognize."

"Thank you," Autumn laughed. "What you think I've been telling him?"

"He'll come around, you'll see," Jaicyn said. "You look hot."

"Especially if you let me rock those black Jimmy Choo sandals I saw in your closet."

Shoes, especially expensive designer shoes, were Jaicyn's weakness. The shoes Autumn was referring to had cost over five hundred dollars and had never been worn. Rayshawn always complained that her shoes and bags were taking over the closet but Jaicyn couldn't help it. Her suggestion for the closet problem was that Rayshawn build another one.

"Girl, you can have those shoes. Consider them my graduation present."

Autumn screeched and ran into Jaicyn's walk-in closet.

"There's a purse in there that matches those shoes. Take that too," Jaicyn yelled after her. She tied a short sheer white wrap around her waist and opened the bedroom door.

"Hurry up!"

Rayshawn was manning the grill full of chicken and ribs when Jaicyn and Autumn reached the pool. He looked good, standing there in his black basketball shorts and no shirt. The heat from the sun combined with the heat from the grill made his dark skin glisten like a melting bar of chocolate.

Jaicyn walked up behind him and put her arms around his waist.

"Hey Sexy," she whispered in his ear.

"You're the sexy one," Rayshawn said, turning around and checked out his woman. "Damn, you look good in that. You're going to make all these chicks here jealous," Rayshawn added.

Jaicyn glanced around their backyard at the few scantily clad woman in bikinis. Even though some of them were her friends, she didn't care if they were jealous. That was the point of her wearing her cutest bathing suit. Jaicyn was quickly becoming one of the best dressed of all the Atlanta fashionistas and her popularity in the Atlanta fashion scene was well deserved.

"It's my house," Jaicyn answered. "I'm supposed to look the best. But look at Autumn. Her bathing suit is amazing. She looks so good."

"I bet she does," Rayshawn laughed. "Dayshawn's here."

Jaicyn laughed too. "Everything good here?" she asked. "You need anything?"

"Can you fix me a drink?" Rayshawn asked. "Hennessy and coke, you know how I like it."

"Coming right up."

Jaicyn headed over to the bar. Rayshawn watched her walk away and noticed a couple of the guys doing the same. Not that he could blame them. His fiancée was the hottest chick at the party. In fact, Jaicyn was probably the hottest chick in Atlanta. All these guys could do was look and be mad that their women didn't have the natural beauty that Jaicyn possessed.

After making sure that her man had everything he needed, Jaicyn settled into her favorite chaise with a strong pomegranate margarita, her sunglasses, and her best friend next to her and watched the crowd. She was determined to fade into the background. She didn't feel like playing hostess. Rayshawn was doing a good enough job.

"I can't believe that Dayshawn already passed the bar?" Autumn said, interrupting Jaicyn's moment of complete relaxation.

"Yeah," she answered. "And that law firm he was interning at offered him a position."

"I know. I'm so proud of him."

Jaicyn sipped her drink and took off her shades to get a better view of her teenage sisters playing chicken in the pool with their friends. She had to keep a watchful eye on them and their male friends. Rickie and Bobbie were teenagers now. Jaicyn knew how hot girls their age could be. She had to watch them.

"I have to tell you something," Autumn said. Jaicyn didn't like the tone of her voice.

"What?"

"I saw your mother a few weeks ago."

"I don't have a mother," Jaicyn replied and kept staring at the pool.

"She asked about you," Autumn said. Jaicyn sat up in her chair and whipped off her sunglasses.

"What did you say? You didn't say anything about us, did you? Please tell me you didn't tell her where we live!"

Autumn shook her head. "I told her you and the girls were doing fine and that's all I could tell her."

Jaicyn sat back and let Autumn's words sink in. She hadn't thought about her mother in years. Rickie and Bobbie never brought her up. In a way, she was dead to them. When Angelina never came to get them from the foster home, she ceased to exist to Rickie and Bobbie. The last time Jaicyn laid eyes on her, she was strung out on crack, far worse than she'd ever been before.

"Do you think you'll ever talk to her again?" Autumn asked.

"Not a chance in hell," Jaicyn stated sharply. "Like I said, I don't have a mother."

"We're doing fine here," Jaicyn added. "Pretty soon, me and Rayshawn are going to be out the game and living like normal folks. I don't need her in my life fucking things up. I can't help that woman, Autumn. I tried. I have my family and my business. That's all I care about now."

Jaicyn was proud of her little business and was eager to expand. If Rayshawn could keep his ass out of jail, she was willing to leave the life they were living and make a fresh start. She just hadn't told him yet.

She was meeting all the right types of people. They had no idea what she did and the story about being a trust fund kid suited Atlanta's elite.

Rayshawn was still was trying to move in a different direction. The moving and storage companies were doing well but he really wanted to work on his record label. Jaicyn knew that they had more than enough money to slip quietly away and live a different life. She only had to convince her fiancé of her plan so he'd stay out of prison.

King made a lot of money and taught Jaicyn well. She also learned from her former boss, Darrius. He taught her a lot about the stock market. While most of their money was hidden in numbered accounts in the Caribbean and in Europe, where their accountants had determined it was safest, what they did keep in the United States was invested in high risk stocks and recycled through their businesses.

"I know you care, Autumn," Jaicyn said. "But can we agree to never talk about her again? She's in the past and I don't want to focus on that."

"Sure. I won't bring her up again."

The girls were quiet. A few times, Jaicyn caught Autumn staring at Dayshawn and smiled.

"Can I just tell you, again, how much I love this house," Autumn sighed. "I can't believe you and Rayshawn managed to do all this without every going to college."

"I have smart people around me," Jaicyn answered humbly. "I figured if Jay-Z can make millions and not set foot on a college campus, so can I. He started out hustling, just like me."

Autumn laughed. "I should have known! Do you remember when you wanted to marry him?"

Of course Jaicyn remembered! He was her dream before Rayshawn came into the picture.

"I can't believe you brought that up."

"But then Rayshawn gave you that cheap pawn shop ring and you dropped poor old Jay-Z," Autumn said.

"Hey," Jaicyn protested, "that ring was special. I still have that ring! Besides, Jay-Z has Beyonce. He don't want me."

The two girls laughed. Jaicyn looked around at the party guests and noticed that someone was missing.

"I wonder where King is. He told the twins that he was coming."

Autumn shrugged her shoulders. "Sandy probably made his ass stay home. I bet my man wouldn't be leaving me in Washington Heights with two kids while he goes to Atlanta to party."

"Well, you better leave that little tidbit on Post-Its and stick them all over your house if you and twin number two get married cause we both know that Dayshawn is not going to pass up a good party!"

"I know, right! So," Autumn said, getting serious, "what's the word on the investigation? Are y'all going to be okay?"

Jaicyn stopped smiling. For the last few months she'd been on edge, wondering the same thing.

"We haven't heard anything," Jaicyn answered. "Dayshawn says that he hasn't heard anything new either."

Autumn sensed that she'd hit a sore spot and hadn't meant to. She just worried about her friends. At the end of the day, no matter how involved Jaicyn was in her boutique, she was still the very much involved girlfriend of a drug dealer. Whatever happened to Rayshawn probably would happen to her. Autumn couldn't imagine Jaicyn spending the rest of her life in prison. What would happen to Rickie and Bobbie?

"Come on," Autumn said to lighten the mood, "let's get in the pool. I didn't buy this swimsuit just to look pretty."

Jaicyn smiled and welcomed the distraction. However, the conversation with Autumn reminded her that she needed to have a separate conversation with her lawyers and fiancé soon. Until then, she was going to enjoy the party going on in her backyard.

CHAPTER 11

Rayshawn heard his cell phone vibrating on the beside table and quickly grabbed it before it woke up Jaicyn who was sleeping beside him. She had a little too much to drink at the party and after a quickie with her man, had passed out on their bed.

Rayshawn was glad that Jaicyn hadn't demanded too much of his attention. He had a lot of things on his mind and Jaicyn had a way making him talk about stuff that he didn't really want to talk about. She wasn't going to like any of the news that he had to give her. How was he supposed to tell her that at any moment, their world was going to be turned upside down?

Rayshawn looked at the caller ID on his phone and hit the talk button. Xavier Rogers was just the call that he'd been waiting all day for.

"Hold on," Rayshawn said into the phone. He got out of the bed and walked quietly to the patio door. Stepping out on the balcony, he saw his brother and Autumn spending some alone time in the pool. It was three in the morning but who was he to judge? Instead, Rayshawn sat on the lounge chair in the shadows so that Dayshawn wouldn't look up and see him.

"What's up X? Rayshawn said into his phone.

Xavier Rogers Jr. was the oldest son of Detroit's most notorious drug kingpin. Rayshawn had met him during one of his and King's many trips to Detroit to link up with the senior Xavier. Xavier reminded Rayshawn of his brother, studious and not interested in the business of selling drugs. Like Dayshawn, he had other plans for his life. He wanted to work for the FBI and two years ago he finally got the chance. Now he was a part of the task force put together to bring down Cesar Valdez and the drug cartel he'd been supplying.

"Things ain't looking too good, brother," Xavier solemnly informed his friend. "I tried everything to take the focus off you but they ain't havin' it."

Rayshawn was expecting the news. In fact, he thought that when Xavier finally called him he'd be saying that the Feds were about to bust through his door. Blaque had called him earlier that morning to let him know that the Washington Heights police and the DEA had raided two of King's territories and arrested Sonny and K-ci. Rayshawn's instincts told him that he was next.

"So what're my options because I know they got me in their sights?" Rayshawn asked.

"You're right," Xavier answered. He didn't want to see his friend go down. He was law enforcement but he still wanted to help Rayshawn and Jaicyn.

"This is the deal," Xavier started to explain. "You have twenty-four hours to turn yourself in."

"Or what?" Rayshawn wanted to know.

"Or they come and get you," Xavier answered gravely. "And if you're not there, they are going to arrest anyone there."

Anyone meant Jaicyn. Rayshawn didn't even need clarification on that one.

On his side of the phone, Rayshawn groaned. He wasn't a punk. He lived by a code and that was 'never confess' and 'never give yourself up. If they want you let them come get you.

"But look," Xavier said, "you know I got your back. I can lose my job or go to jail for this, but I took care of things for you. You know, talked to some people, got rid of some evidence. They really don't have anything that your lawyers can't beat. They are hoping that once you get in the box and they start threatening your family, you'll start to talk."

Rayshawn snickered. That would never happen. He wasn't a snitch. Plus he knew that Xavier would come through for him. He might have been a cop but he was from the streets. He'd look out for his own people before anything else.

"Look, tell your people that I'll turn myself in as long as they leave Jaicyn alone. They start fuckin' with her and they'll never find us."

Xavier knew that Rayshawn would set his own terms when it came down to it. He also knew that Rayshawn would sacrifice his own life and freedom for his fiancée. Maybe the FBI didn't realize it but everyone who really knew Rayshawn and Jaicyn knew it. Rayshawn was a rock and he'd never turn on King or Cesar.

Because the FEDS had made a horrible assumption about Rayshawn, an assumption that Xavier had perpetuated. Xavier knew that Rayshawn would come out okay. He'd have to do some jail time when he didn't give up the information that the agents were expecting him to, but that was a given.

"I'll tell them I'll bring you in," Xavier suggested. "What you gon do about Jaicyn?"

Rayshawn looked into the bedroom where Jaicyn was still sleeping. The moonlight cast a soft light into the bedroom, just enough so that he could see his woman. Rayshawn felt a slight a pull at his heart, knowing that once again they'd be separated for an unspecified amount of time.

"Jaicyn will be alright. She's a soldier."

"Yeah," Xavier had to agree. "She'll hold you down for sure."

Rayshawn nodded. After making a promise to call him the next day, Rayshawn hung up the phone and stared over the balcony. He was tempted to holler down to the pool and tell his brother to come in the house but he chose not to. He was already about to ruin Jaicyn's night. He could at least wait until his brother got some before ruining his day too. He slid open the patio door and slipped back into the bed next to Jaicyn.

"Who was on the phone?" Jaicyn asked as soon as Rayshawn sat on the bed.

"What?"

Jaicyn sat up on the bed and switched on the light.

"Who was on the phone," she repeated. "What was so important that you had to go outside and talk to them at three in the morning?"

"Xavier," Rayshawn answered.

Jaicyn rolled her eyes. "I don't know any damn Xavier."

"Yes you do," Rayshawn replied. "Xavier from Detroit."

"Are you talking about the cop?"

Rayshawn nodded. Jaicyn looked into his eyes and knew something was wrong.

"What did he want?" she asked slowly, even though she knew. She just had to hear it for herself.

Over the last few days Jaicyn had noticed that Rayshawn had been quieter and more withdrawn than ever. While she was worried about the federal investigation, she had to put on a happy face for her sisters. Rayshawn didn't know how to do that. When Rayshawn told her that Xavier was the late night caller, Jaicyn's stomach churned.

"What's going on Rayshawn? What did he say?"

Rayshawn took a deep breath and put his arm around his fiancée.

"They're making moves," he said. "They raided 91st Street and Oakland Terrace last night and the reason why King didn't come to the party is because he's in Bermuda."

"Then we're getting the hell out of dodge too," Jaicyn interrupted. "When are we leaving?"

"We're not," Rayshawn answered gravely. "Baby, we can't leave now. It's too late."

Jaicyn found it hard to believe what Rayshawn was saying. It was never too late to leave. She got out of bed and ran over to the patio door. She looked around the lawn and didn't see anything but shadows.

"I don't see the police out there about to bust down our door. So if they're not out there then it's not too late."

"Baby, it's too late," Rayshawn said again. "Did you hear what I said about Washington Heights?"

Jaicyn wasn't dumb. She knew how to put two and two together. If Sonny and K-ci were locked up and King was on the run, then all eyes were on Rayshawn. How long had he'd known?

"Rayshawn, you have two seconds to tell me why we can't get the hell out of here! We have enough money to go anywhere in this world that we want to go. Why should we stay here and wait for them to lock us up?" Jaicyn yelled.

"Because I'm not living my life on the run, that's why. Whatever shit these dumb ass cops throw at me, I can beat," Rayshawn explained with as much confidence as he could muster. But Jaicyn wasn't buying his story. He was worried and so was she.

"Don't give me that bullshit," Jaicyn snarled at her man. "Yeah, we might be able to beat a drug charge but we don't know if they have anything else, do we? That's a totally different story. We should just go."

Rayshawn knew that Jaicyn wasn't worried about beating drug charges. She had the murders of Mario, Ramel, and his crew on her mind. But Rayshawn figured that Xavier would have told him if they had murder charges on him. Murder was more serious that drugs. Xavier was doing more than risking his career. Blaque and Slim knew that he was helping Rayshawn. Not telling Rayshawn that the FEDS had murder charges would have been risking his life.

Rayshawn looked at Jaicyn. She was about to cry. He knew that she'd be upset and he'd figured that she'd cry. He just hated doing that to her. It was inevitable though.

"Baby," Rayshawn said and put his arm around Jaicyn. He pulled her close to him. "We're going to be alright. They know nothing about that. We're straight."

"I just don't understand," Jaicyn cried with her head against Rayshawn's chest. "We can leave here and not have to worry about this shit."

Rayshawn didn't have the right words to explain that he couldn't leave the country because he'd never ask her to give up everything for him again. He wouldn't allow her to give up her boutique and her friends. He didn't want Rickie and Bobbie to have to live like fugitives. No, if leaving was an option then it would only be an option for him.

"Jay-Jay, I'm going to beat these charges, whatever they are. We know how tight our shit is. I'm not worried and if I'm not worried then you shouldn't be either," Rayshawn assured her.

"What am I supposed to do without you?" Jaicyn whined and hugged Rayshawn tightly.

"The same thing I did without you for two years, maintained."

With her head on Rayshawn shoulders, Jaicyn fingered her engagement ring and toughened up.

"I can do that," she said. "How long do you think you'll be gone?"

Rayshawn shrugged. "Who knows? Maybe a few months, I don't know. But I have twenty-four hours to turn myself in.

Rayshawn placed his hand under Jaicyn's chin and raised her head so that she was looking directly into his eyes.

"I need you to be strong and believe that we're going to get through this. I need you to be the rock that I know you are. You and I are too strong to be defeated, baby. We always have been and we always will be."

"I know," Jaicyn answered. All traces of her tears were gone. "I got you, Rayshawn."

Rayshawn felt better hearing her say those words. He and Jaicyn had been through too much bad stuff in their short lives. Good things were just starting to happen. It wouldn't be right for things to come to an end like this. Plus they'd always been more secretive, crafty, and careful than all of the other dealers they knew.

When Rayshawn hooked up with Xavier in a grocery store parking lot the next day he wasn't scared or nervous. He just wanted to get it over with. The summer was just starting and he had more important things to tend to. Plus he couldn't leave Jaicyn alone to plan their wedding for too long.

CHAPTER 12

Jaicyn sat in the cold waiting room of the Dekalb County Jail looking around at all of the visitors waiting to have a brief thirty minute visit with their husbands, fathers, sons, and boyfriends. She hated coming to the jail. Seeing all of the crying babies, lonely wives, pissed off girlfriends, and heartbroken mothers was depressing. Every Tuesday, Thursday, and Saturday Jaicyn dreaded getting dressed in plain jeans, a t-shirt, and sneakers and making the drive down Memorial Drive to the jail. She did it because Rayshawn needed her to. Three times a week for the last five months Jaicyn visited her fiancé in jail.

Rayshawn was doing okay. Jaicyn was the one struggling to hold herself together. She was unprepared, mentally, to deal with her man being locked up for any length of time. It was her own fault. She knew that jail was always a possibility but she'd gotten comfortable. The longing to live a normal life had made her forget how she actually made her money.

Now, here they were; she on the outside preparing for Rayshawn's trial while he sat behind bars. Nothing in the last few months had gone the way Jaicyn expected it to; the smooth way Rayshawn had promised. No one in Washington Heights, not even Blaque or Sandy would return her calls. Her man was facing serious charges including drug trafficking and money laundering. The FEDS had seized their house and their cars. They even froze the money in their bank account. Still, the only people who talked to her were Dayshawn and Autumn.

Even when the judge denied Rayshawn's bail, no one answered the phone. Jaicyn was more irritated than hurt. Rayshawn would be hurt if he found out. She wouldn't let him. He needed to focus on the twenty years he was facing, not what was going on in Washington Heights.

Jaicyn was so absorbed in her thoughts that she almost missed the stony faced clerk call her name. Like an old pro, Jaicyn walked through the door and took the elevator up to the fourth floor visitation room. She took a seat behind the glass partition and waited for Rayshawn to enter on the other side. Only one other person was inside the room with Jaicyn, a sad Hispanic woman Jaicyn had seen before. The older woman was just as diligent in visiting her eighteen year old son as Jaicyn was in visiting Rayshawn. Sometimes Jaicyn would give the lady a ride home so she wouldn't have to take the bus after a visit with her son.

In his orange jumpsuit, Rayshawn still looked quite handsome. He still had that confidant swagger Jaicyn adored. Jaicyn waited until he sat down behind the glass before picking up the phone.

"Hey baby," she greeted him. "What's up?"

Rayshawn smiled back. "What's up?"

Jail, especially county jail, was tolerable as long as he minded his own business. His reputation on the streets had followed him to jail. He was Dekalb County Jail's resident celebrity of sorts. Most of the guys on the tier were locked up for drugs and guns. Any drug dealer in Atlanta that was making good money by selling the 'good shit' was probably getting dope from Rayshawn in one way or another so no one bothered him.

Rayshawn had gotten used to the routine of jail, but he missed his fiancé and his brother in a major way. Even though they both visited regularly, Rayshawn needed to be free to take care of them.

"How you doing?" Rayshawn asked.

"I'm okay," was Jaicyn's answer.

"And the girls?"

"They're fine. They don't like the apartment," Jaicyn added. "But they still haven't released our house or cars."

"Baby, we're probably never going to get that shit back," Rayshawn replied angrily. "It's gone."

Jaicyn stared through the Plexiglas at the dingy wall behind Rayshawn. She didn't want to believe that he was right. Her house, her dream house, couldn't just be snatched away from her.

"Jay-Jay," Rayshawn said into the phone, "you're not holding it together."

"I'm trying," she snapped. "But you're in here and I'm out there in a tiny ass apartment, driving a fucking Honda Civic, a used Honda Civic!" she hissed. "You're in here and I'm out there pretending that I can't live better than that. This is fucking bullshit!"

Rayshawn laughed. Only Jaicyn would complain about driving a used car. She'd gotten spoiled. The knock the FEDS gave her back into reality was good for her.

"You know why you're doing this," Rayshawn insisted.

"I know," Jaicyn heaved a deep sigh.

She could have bought a brand new house and more cars the same day hers was taken but their lawyers warned her not to. They had to pretend like they didn't have any money, except what she made from *Caliente*.

Living on a budget again was hard after not worrying abut money for ten years. She had to readjust and she was not happy about it.

"My lawyers are coming up later," Rayshawn told her. "They set my trial date."

Jaicyn's eyes widened. Thank God! "When?"

"Next month. On the twentieth."

"Good."

"When I beat this shit, I should be home by Thanksgiving," Rayshawn said confidently.

Jaicyn nodded. She wouldn't get her hopes up. The lawyers told her not to. No one knew how long the trial would last. Plus a not guilty verdict on all charges was unlikely. As much as she hated to hear them talk about the possibility of Rayshawn not getting out, Jaicyn had finally started to come to terms with the reality of the situation. Rayshawn might be gone for a few years.

"What's wrong?" Rayshawn asked. He didn't understand the sullen look on Jaicyn's face.

"Nothing," Jaicyn mumbled. She had no intention of getting Rayshawn upset. She may have spoken freely if the situation was different but Jaicyn only had thirty minutes to spend with the man she loved and he didn't need to be burdened with her emotional baggage. She was sure that he had enough of his own.

"So, what's Dayshawn saying? Are they prepared to start trial so soon?" Jaicyn asked quietly, desperately trying to change the subject because she didn't want her man to know how she was really feeling.

Rayshawn frowned. Behind the make-up Jaicyn had expertly applied, Rayshawn knew that she was scared. Her hazel eyes didn't sparkle anymore. But what could he do? What Jaicyn was feeling was reality.

Seeing him behind the glass made her realize what life would be like without him.

"Rayshawn," Jaicyn snapped, "answer me."

Rayshawn snapped back to attention after letting his mind wander. "What?"

"What is Dayshawn saying about his law firm?" Jaicyn repeated. "Are they going to be ready for trial?"

"We don't talk about that kind of stuff when I see him," Rayshawn answered. "He's not involved with my case."

"He's not involved in your case? Why the hell not?"

"Because," Rayshawn uttered. "He's never been caught up in this shit before and I don't want him starting now."

Jaicyn couldn't believe what he was saying. Dayshawn was lucky enough to get hired at the same law firm where she and Rayshawn retained the best lawyers in Atlanta. It made sense for him to be involved, especially now. His brother needed him more than ever. How could he just stay on the sidelines and watch them lock his brother up for the rest of his life.

Jaicyn wanted an explanation but Rayshawn wouldn't give her one. Dayshawn wasn't happy with his decision either. They both had to get over it.

"But Rayshawn," Jaicyn started to protest but Rayshawn stopped her.

"There's nothing to talk about. His first real case is not going to be mine! He's not going to ruin his career before it even gets started."

"That's stupid," Jaicyn fought to get the last word in. "He's your brother! He should be helping you."

"I'm paying enough people to help me," Rayshawn growled. "So don't even worry about that. Why don't you and the girls go visit your father or your grandmother? Try to relax or something. I need you on your game, baby."

"I am on my game," Jaicyn argued. "Ask Raul and Cortez how much on my game I am. Nothing's fucking changed."

Rayshawn bristled at the mention of the Valdez brothers. Jaicyn knew better to speak their names into a jail phone.

"What the fuck, Jay-Jay? What are you trying to do?"

"Sorry," Jaicyn said after she realized her mistake.

"You can't be making those stupid mistakes. I'm trying to get out this motherfucker, not get caught up in some more shit. You're slippin'."

Jaicyn's expression hardened. She was slippin'. She was so tired of having to take care of everything herself! But she had to. She had to keep them afloat while Rayshawn was locked down.

"It won't happen again," she promised. "I got you, baby."

"That's all I needed to hear," Rayshawn grinned slightly.

Jaicyn looked at her watch. Their thirty minutes were almost up and the phone would cut off in mid-sentence if she and Rayshawn didn't say goodbye soon.

"Well," Jaicyn said slowly, "I gotta go. Are you going to call me after you meet with your lawyers?"

"I'll try but it depends on what's going on here and how late it is. I might not be able to get a phone."

"Alright," Jaicyn said, crossing her fingers that he'd be able to get to a phone. She hated the days when he didn't call and their thirty minute visits had to suffice.

"Jay-Jay," Rayshawn said, noticing the disappointment in Jaicyn's voice, "be strong. I love you."

"I love you too."

They had an unspoken rule that they always ended their visit on their own, never waiting for some unseen guard with too much power to pull the plug on their conversation. Instead their visit ended about two minutes before it was supposed to when Rayshawn got up and walked to the door, waiting to be escorted back to his tier.

Jaicyn drove straight to Dayshawn's office after leaving the jail. She wanted to talk to about him abandoning his brother. Even if Rayshawn didn't want him to be directly involved, Dayshawn should have insisted on it. Rayshawn was sitting in jail, facing enough drug charges that could put him away for twenty years. None of this made any sense.

Jaicyn entered the law firm, bypassed the receptionist, and walked straight into Dayshawn's small office on the third floor. He was on the phone and motioned for her to have a seat. Jaicyn closed the door and sat down in one of the two Herman Miller desk chairs.

Rayshawn's lawyers were housed on the fifteenth floor where the senior partners' suite of offices were. There were four offices up there, some of the most fantastic and beautifully designed offices Dayshawn had ever seen. Dayshawn had only been to the fifteenth floor one time, and that was for his final interview. He rarely seen the partners in the six months he'd been working there. All he knew that the four partners worked the toughest and notorious cases that the firm had. They had their own elevator to their suites and hardly anyone saw them. But an email from one of the four partners would throw floors one through fourteen into a frenzy.

Dayshawn, in his black suit, light purple shirt, and purple and silver tie, already looked the part of the senior partner that he wanted to be, at least in Jaicyn's opinion. Now that his business card finally read Dayshawn Moore, Attorney at Law, women were lined up around the block to get a taste of the fine chocolate specimen who filled out a tailored suit better than Morris Chestnut.

Autumn better stop bullshittin' and snatch this boy up, Jaicyn thought to herself.

"What's up, Jaicyn?" Dayshawn asked after he hung up the phone.

"I just got back from visiting Rayshawn," Jaicyn replied. "Did you know he goes to court next month?"

Dayshawn nodded. He'd gotten an email from the lead attorney on Rayshawn's case, Michael Woodruff, earlier that morning.

"Why aren't you on the team?" Jaicyn demanded to know.

"Can't. Rayshawn doesn't want me to," Dayshawn explained quickly.

"That's bullshit," Jaicyn argued. "Why wouldn't you work your brother's case? Don't give me that 'he told me not to' bullshit. This is one of those times when you can ignore what he says."

"No, I can't. Rayshawn is a paying client. The firm will do what he wants. He doesn't even want me in the courtroom, but I'm not going to do that."

"Rayshawn is on some bullshit," Jaicyn replied. "We're both going to be in the courtroom."

"Have you talked to Sandy or King?" Dayshawn changed the subject.

Jaicyn shook her head.

"Me either."

The coldness in Dayshawn's voice caught Jaicyn's attention. Of course he was pissed over that. They were family and the Carters had turned their backs on them. The last thing Jaicyn heard was that Sandy and the kids had joined King in Bermuda.

"I can't believe he left my brother out there like that. He knew this shit was coming," Dayshawn said angrily. "He knew and didn't even warn us."

"That's the game," Jaicyn shrugged. "It happens all the time. I don't know why you and your brother thought King was any different. I told you that he was going to do this, but no one ever fuckin' listens to me. But we're smarter than King," she continued. "At least, I am. We're going to be alright."

"I hope so."

"I know so." Jaicyn's words were a hundred times more confident than she looked. Dayshawn wondered what she was thinking but from the look on her face, she wasn't about to tell him.

"You should take me to lunch," he suggested instead.

"No can do, *papi*. I have to get to the shop and make some money since it's my only source of income," she laughed. "But stop by later. I'm making fajitas."

"Sounds like a plan."

When Jaicyn left the law office she felt a little better. Dayshawn hadn't really turned his back on his brother like the crew back home had done. She was pissed that she couldn't depend on any of them for anything, not even a little support. They'd made millions together and now they were acting like complete strangers.

Jaicyn respected King's position in Washington Heights. He was the boss. She didn't want anything bad to happen to him. Unlike Rayshawn, she didn't have a special bond with him. He was her employer. When the shit hit the fan, she knew that they'd have to fend for themselves. Drugs were a dirty game. And King had never played fair. To him, his people, Rayshawn included, were just casualties of war.

King had pulled a disappearing act. He thought he was safe in Bermuda with his wife and kids. Jaicyn figured that King was counting on Rayshawn to keep his mouth shut, which he would. Rayshawn would do some years and King would continue to make money. But Jaicyn had a different plan.

Her man wasn't going to stay locked up for the rest of his life like K-ci and Sonny. He wasn't going on the run like King. She had access to their money and was willing to put all of it to good use if necessary. She'd already talked to the only man who was powerful enough to help her. If it started to look like Rayshawn was going to lose his case, Jaicyn was willing to pay off the judge, prosecutor or jurors to make sure Rayshawn didn't spend his life behind bars. Her plan B was risky but if all else failed, Cesar was waiting on her call.

CHAPTER 13

Jaicyn walked into the federal courthouse wearing a brand new Chanel pantsuit and her sunglasses. Dayshawn walked beside her. Today was the last day of Rayshawn's ten day trial. He was taking the stand today.

Rayshawn sat next to his attorneys looking every bit as calm as some waiting on the bus, although he was tired of it all. He got angrier each day that the prosecutor tried to present her weak ass case. With barely any evidence and no legit witnesses, Michael Woodruff had basically torn their case to shreds.

Rayshawn winked at his fiancée as he walked to the witness box. He glared at the prosecutor before he sat down. He hated that bitch. He wanted nothing more than to slap the shit out of her when she told the jury about the day his father shot his mom and how that incident had led to Rayshawn's supposed life of crime.

"Rayshawn," Michael said from his place behind the defense table. "Have you ever sold drugs?"

"Yes," Rayshawn admitted. "I did when I was a teenager."

"When did you stop?"

"Right after I moved to Atlanta with my fiancée."

"Are you currently associated with any known drug dealers?"

Rayshawn snickered. "Yeah. All of my friends back home."

"And who would that be?"

Rayshawn began making up nicknames. "Quan, T-dogg, Lil Jo. But I don't get home much."

"Do you know Andre Carter or Cesar Valdez?"

Rayshawn shook his head. "Never met them," he lied easily.

"Ladies and gentleman," Woodruff said to the jury. "My client is a good kid that made a mistake when he was a kid. All the prosecution has proven is that he lived in a city supposedly run by a drug kingpin and that he sold drugs in that city for a few years. Rayshawn just admitted that. I have no further questions."

The female prosecutor marched over to the witness stand and stood directly in front of Rayshawn.

"Mr. Moore, the FBI seized two forty thousand dollar cars, a house in your name valued at over four hundred thousand dollars, and almost seven hundred thousand dollars in assets in your name. How does a twenty-five year old afford such luxuries with no verifiable income?"

"My fiancée and I have three successful businesses and like I said, I sold dope for five years. I was smart with my money."

"You expect this jury to believe that?"

"Why not? Look at that Facebook guy. He's a billionaire and he's my age. It's possible to be young with money, if you're smart."

"Have you gone to college? Do you have a degree in business or finance that the court doesn't know about," she persisted.

"Don't need one," Rayshawn answered. "I didn't have to go to college to learn about the stock market. They write books about it. Anyone with a little common sense can hire a broker."

As she continued her line of questioning, the prosecutor was getting frustrated. She knew that Rayshawn was lying through his teeth. After seeing the tapes of his police interviews, she hadn't even wanted to bring such a weak case to trial. He was smart. He was charming, and he could lie his butt off.

But the federal government didn't like being outsmarted by a thug from the streets. They wanted to force him to give up his connection. When he didn't budge, they trumped up the charges to scare him into talking. It hadn't worked.

On paper the boy was clean as a whistle. His lawyers, the most expensive firm in Atlanta, had even convinced the judge and jury that they were taking his case pro bono. Her only hope was his girlfriend, but her argument was lost on her bosses. There were direct orders coming down from *somewhere* that Jaicyn Jones was not to be touched. Without going after Jaicyn, there was no way she could win.

"I have nothing else for the defendant," she finally told the judge after listening to Rayshawn answer five more questions with lies she couldn't prove.

She eyed Rayshawn as he strolled over to the defense table. She shook her head slowly. How did two kids from the streets manage to do what he and his girlfriend had just done? Their money was hidden, his fake source of income appeared legit, and he paid taxes. The prosecutor was sure that he was being advised by Cesar Valdez, a hunch she couldn't prove either.

When Michael and the other attorneys finished their closing arguments, Rayshawn knew that the half million dollars that he paid Woodruff and Associates was well spent. When the judge handed the case over to the jury, Rayshawn looked at his fiancée and brother and smiled. It would be over soon. There was no way he could lose.

While the jury deliberated, Michael Woodruff and Paul Collins, the best defense lawyers in Atlanta, treated Jaicyn and Dayshawn to lunch at Benihanna's. Benihana's was still Jaicyn and Rayshawn's favorite restaurant and Jaicyn regaled the group with stories of her and Rayshawn's first trip to the infamous restaurant when they first started dating in Washington Heights.

"So, what do you think is going to happen when we go back in there?" Jaicyn asked, turning serious.

Paul wiped his mouth with the white cloth napkin and took a sip of his martini. Paul was the youngest partner at the firm. He was also one of the most convincing people Jaicyn had ever met. He was the one who convinced Michael to bring on Rayshawn's brother as an intern and then as a junior associate. He was closest, as close as a lawyer could be, to Rayshawn and Jaicyn.

"I think that the jury will deliberate for a little longer so they can have a free lunch courtesy of the state of Georgia. Then they're going to come back with a not guilty verdict. They have nothing to go on and did you see that jury? Eight blacks, two white women, and two Hispanics. They are not going to convict, you can be sure of that."

Jaicyn was glad that Paul was so sure. Michael looked confident too. Only Jaicyn was unsure. She wasn't a lawyer. She thought the prosecutor presented a good case. Thank goodness they never mentioned any of the murders or shootings that Rayshawn had been involved in. Xavier made sure that the information stayed buried in the streets of Washington Heights.

The foursome finished lunch around two o'clock. The law firm was right around the corner so the three lawyers went back to work while waiting for the call that the jury had come in. Jaicyn didn't have anything to do so she caught the MARTA train to Centennial Park and walked around, reflecting on everything that had happened in her life since she hooked up with Rayshawn.

They'd done a lot of shit and it was finally catching up with them. They were a part of the biggest drug operation in the Midwest. They'd come so close to losing everything, including Rayshawn's freedom. If Rayshawn got off, they had to get out. She didn't care about the money. Money wasn't important anymore. It was time to walk away.

An hour later, Dayshawn called to let her know the jury was back and the lawyers were heading to the courthouse. Jaicyn grabbed a cab back to the courthouse because she didn't want to risk taking the train and missing the verdict. Stepping into the courthouse, Jaicyn took Dayshawn's hand and squeezed it tightly as they walked into the courtroom.

Her palm was sweaty and her leg started to twitch when Rayshawn was led back to the defense table by the bailiff. He looked at the nervous expression on Jaicyn's face and shook his head. He hadn't wanted her there when the verdict was read and thought that he had been very clear with his lawyers when he said for them to keep her out of the courtroom. Obviously Jaicyn was more persistent than he thought.

After ordering the court to maintain a level of order once the verdict was read, the judge, a mean looking black man who at one time may have been good looking but now just resembled Clarence Thomas, allowed the jury to enter the courtroom.

"Has the jury reached a verdict," Judge Vaughn asked the foreman, a middle aged Black man who ran his own lawn care service.

"Yes sir, we have."

"Please read it."

The foreman took a slip of paper out of his blazer pocket and adjusted his reading glasses.

"We the jury, find the defendant, Rayshawn Moore, not guilty on all charges." The foreman smiled and handed the paper to the bailiff who then handed it over to the judge. He read it over carefully while Jaicyn closed her eyes and practically sat on her hands to keep from screaming for joy.

Judge Vaughn looked at Rayshawn. "Young man, with a verdict of not guilty on all charges, you are free to go."

Rayshawn's smile was smug. He walked past the prosecutor and shook his head. She turned away, embarrassed that she'd been outsmarted by him. He was free to continue selling drugs to whoever he wanted and she was powerless to stop it, unless she could convince her bosses to keep the case going. She'd get him and his connections, one day.

Rayshawn turned to his fiancée and motioned for her to come closer. Jaicyn practically jumped into his arms. He promptly wiped away the tears from her eyes.

"No tears," he ordered. "I told you everything was going to be alright. Now let's get the hell out of here."

CHAPTER 14

Rayshawn felt Jaicyn shift beside him and grinned when she slid her leg over his and invaded his side of the bed. There was enough space on her side, but every night she ended up with her legs and arms entangled with him and he on the edge of the bed.

He'd missed that.

After spending six months in county jail, sleeping in his own bed with his fiancée felt better than he ever imagined it would. He slipped his arm around her bare waist and pulled Jaicyn as close to his body as possible. The La Perla lingerie that she'd worn for about two point five seconds lay at the foot of the bed. As sexy as she looked in the black French lace, the outfit hadn't been necessary...for either of them. They'd made love all night and the sun was starting to rise.

Rickie and Bobbie would be getting ready for school in a few minutes. Rayshawn listened for Rickie's alarm clock. He wanted to talk to both of them before they left. He knew that they hated having to leave their big house in Stone Mountain and put most of their stuff in storage. He remembered what it felt like when he and Dayshawn had to downsize so they could go live in their grandparents' small house. He wanted to apologize.

Jaicyn didn't stir when Rayshawn eased out of the bed. He gently closed their bedroom door behind him and walked down the short hallway to Rickie and Bobbie's room. Both girls were sitting on their beds watching the Weather Channel before deciding on their outfit for the day.

"Is Jaicyn up?" Bobbie asked him. "Because she said she would drive us to school."

"I'll take you," Rayshawn volunteered. "Let her sleep."

"I don't se why we have to go to school today anyway," Rickie complained.

"Why shouldn't you?"

"Because you just came home! We haven't seen you in six months. That's a reason to skip school."

If there was a chance that she could get out of going to school, Rickie was going to milk it for all it was worth. She was like Jaicyn in that way.

"Nah," Rayshawn shook his head. "We'll kick it this weekend. But I want to talk to you though."

"About what?"

Rayshawn sat down on Bobbie's pink and purple comforter. The girls sat next to him. He looked serious. They waited patiently for him to speak.

"I want to apologize to you guys," Rayshawn said. "I should have planned better. I didn't think they'd take the house. If I had known that, I'd have got another house for you guys."

"It's not that bad," Bobbie started to say but Rickie stopped her.

"No, the apartment isn't that bad," Rickie agreed, "but is this how it's always going to be?"

Rayshawn looked at her. "What do you mean?"

"I mean," Rickie sighed. "We had the townhouse in Washington Heights, and then we had to stay in the foster home. Then we moved into the condo with Jay-Jay, then down here into another apartment. Then we finally get settled into a house and all of a sudden we have to move again. I know what you and Jaicyn do, but do either of you understand how this affects us?"

"Every time we move," Rickie continued, "we have to change neighborhoods and change schools. I'm tired of it. Is this how it's going to be until we go to college?"

"No," Rayshawn answered, suddenly aware that he'd let Rickie and Bobbie down in more ways than one.

He'd been so worried about making sure they had everything that they wanted, he forgot about what they actually needed…stability.

"I'm sorry, girls," he said. "I promise to do better. I moved you here with me to make sure you had a better life, but it hasn't been better, has it?"

"In a way it has," Bobbie replied. "But you and Jaicyn are hardly here and when you got locked up, we were on our own a lot."

"We worry about you and Jaicyn," Rickie added. "It's nice to have money and all, but what if you get locked up or shot? What if something happens to my sister? I don't want to sound like an old person, but you and Jaicyn have to stop."

Rayshawn nodded. He spent six months in jail thinking about his future and the future of the girls he cared about. He didn't want this life for them anymore.

"It's not easy," Rayshawn explained. "But I'm working on it. I promise, the three of you are my only priority. I'm not going to let anything happen to Jaicyn or my little sisters."

He put an arm around each of the girls and hugged them. They hugged him back.

"Get dressed quickly," he said, standing up. "We'll stop and get breakfast before school. I think it'll be okay if you missed first period."

"Cool!" Bobbie cheered.

Rayshawn closed their bedroom door and walked right into Jaicyn. She was leaning against the wall, clutching her robe closed. There were tears in her eyes.

"What's wrong?" Rayshawn asked her.

"I don't know," Jaicyn said, wiping her eyes. "I heard what you said to my sisters. I appreciate that you care so much about them."

"Why wouldn't I? We've practically raised them. They're my responsibility too. Not just yours."

"We haven't been doing a very good job, have we?" Jaicyn muttered sadly. "They were so scared when King got shot, then you got locked up. They worry about us."

Rayshawn leaned back against the wall and stared at the ceiling. "How do we do this?" he asked his partner in crime. "How do we get out? No one has ever just walked away from King's crew. Not without repercussions."

"I don't know," Jaicyn said again. "But we never committed to this for life. We walk away and King has nothing to worry about. We aren't rats. He can trust us."

"We'll see," was all Rayshawn said.

Jaicyn threw her hands in the air and started down the hall. Rayshawn was useless to talk to if the subject matter involved King.

"By the way," she said over her shoulder. "He called. I told him it was your first day home and you'll talk to him next week. If he calls again today, I'm changing our numbers."

Rayshawn knew that Jaicyn was still mad at King and everyone else in Washington Heights. She had to learn how to let shit go. Everything worked out fine. If he didn't care, neither should she.

****

"Hey Jaicyn," Renee called from across the shop. "Phone's for you."

Jaicyn looked up from the stack of real estate listings she'd printed off the Internet. Finding a location for Caliente II was easy. Finding a location for Rayshawn's record label and recording studio was proving to be much harder. But she volunteered. She had an eye for real estate after working for Darrius for so long. Besides, Rayshawn wasn't going to do it.

"Who is it?" Jaicyn yelled back.

"She said her name is Sandy. Want me to tell her you're busy?"

"No, I'll take it," Jaicyn grumbled. She took the cordless phone out of Renee's hand and walked into the manager's office in the back of the store. Her nostrils flared as she slammed the door.

"What?" she snapped into the phone.

"You're a hard person to reach," Sandy laughed. "I've been calling you for two weeks."

"And I've been ignoring you for two weeks," Jaicyn fired back. "Why are you trying to talk to me now? You ignored my calls for six months. What the fuck do you want now?"

"That wasn't personal, Jay-Jay," Sandy started to say but was interrupted.

"Wasn't personal my ass!" Jaicyn yelled. "You and the rest of them left me and Rayshawn down here to fend for ourselves. Don't tell me that was just business, not when we're supposed to be better than that."

Jaicyn lowered her voice a few octaves. "When your man got shot, I was there for you. I took care of that for you. My man gets knocked by the FEDS and you didn't even answer your fuckin' phone. I don't have shit to say to you!"

"Andre wants to see you," Sandy said evenly before Jaicyn could hang up.

"I don't care."

"Jaicyn…" Sandy sighed. "Don't do that."

"Don't do what? Did you get the memo? I don't work for him anymore. We don't owe him anything and we're out. Don't call me again."

Jaicyn hadn't actually discussed it with Rayshawn but she knew he wanted out just as much as she did. Sandy was the perfect messenger.

"It doesn't work like that," Sandy warned. "You know better than that. He'll be there tonight. He's flying private and will be at the Marriott Marquise downtown at eleven. You and Rayshawn need to meet him at the bar at eleven-thirty."

Sandy disconnected the call. Jaicyn stared at the phone briefly before slamming it on the charger. Who the hell did Sandy think she was? All she ever did was follow King around and run her little restaurant. She didn't give orders. She couldn't. She was just married to King. That's it.

She'd sounded so morbid on the phone. "Be there or else" was the impression that Jaicyn got, but she really didn't care. She knew why King wanted to meet and it wasn't a personal visit. Rayshawn must have told him that he wanted out. King was going to try to convince him to stay and

Jaicyn wasn't having it. King and his wife could kiss her ass. King may have been the boss, but she was the boss of her family. He couldn't control them.

****

King was sitting at the hotel bar when he spotted Jaicyn and Rayshawn walking towards him at eleven forty-five that evening. He smiled when they caught his eye. They didn't smile back. They kept the same scowl on their faces as they walked towards him holding hands.

A united front.

He got up and walked to an empty table where they couldn't be overheard easily. The pair followed.

"You wanted to see us," Jaicyn stated as she slid into the booth. It wasn't a question.

"How have you two been holding up?" King asked.

Jaicyn huffed and rolled her eyes.

"We're fine," Rayshawn answered sharply. "How was Bermuda?"

"I wasn't on vacation," King reminded them.

"Yeah, neither was Rayshawn," Jaicyn replied. Rayshawn shook his head at her. Jaicyn's smart mouth wasn't going to make the meeting any easier.

"That's part of why I'm here," King said. "I need to know how you beat a federal drug case. That shit just doesn't happen."

Rayshawn stiffened in his seat. "What are you saying?"

"K-ci, Sonny, and Little Man are all locked up. But you're free. I need to know how that happened."

"I have good lawyers," Rayshawn answered. "Xavier from Detroit helped. Dayshawn knew a lot of shit too."

"Plus we're not stupid like them," Jaicyn added. "That's why you sent us down here instead of them. Because we're careful and smart. Doesn't take a genius to hide money in places the FEDS can't find."

"That's all?" King's tone was skeptical. "You're free because you're smart? That's your explanation?"

"That's the truth," Rayshawn replied. "Take it or leave it. I walked because of my lawyers and my brother. K-ci and Sonny are still locked up because they'd rather spend their money on cars and rims than pay a good lawyer."

"He didn't snitch," Jaicyn stated, "if that's what you're implying. If he had snitched, then we wouldn't be having this meeting because you'd be locked up. Why does any of that matter now? We're done."

King shook his head. "No, you're not done. No one just walks away. With K-ci and Sonny out for good, you two are all I got."

"I don't want to do this anymore," Rayshawn told his boss. "There are plenty of people up there that do. Replace us."

"No."

"No?" Rayshawn repeated.

"You heard me. You two aren't walking away from this because you got scared. You're my supplier down here. This deal we have with Cesar ends when I say it ends."

Jaicyn raised her eyebrows and stared defiantly at King.

"We're done," she clenched her teeth as she spoke. "That last shipment was it for us. We want out."

"What you want doesn't matter," King spoke authoritatively. "You work for me and I make the decisions. Until I find a suitable replacement, you will keep doing things the way they've always been done. Don't cross me on this."

Rayshawn stared across the table. He let go of Jaicyn's hand before he squeezed it too hard and hurt her. He knew that King wasn't happy about him giving up his spot in the crew, but Rayshawn thought they were close enough for King to understand his choice.

"Don't look at me like that," King said to Rayshawn. "Don't act like you're different than anybody else who works for me. I make the rules. There are no exceptions," he continued. "Not even for you. Don't forget, you wanted this. You came to me, remember?"

"I was fifteen," Rayshawn answered. "I didn't sign up for this shit for the rest of my life."

"Sure you did," King chuckled. "We all did."

He stood up and patted Rayshawn's shoulders. "Don't hate me, hate the game," he said before strolling out of the bar.

Jaicyn stared in his direction until she couldn't see him anymore. "What the fuck just happened?"

Rayshawn shrugged his shoulders and balled his hands into fists. "I don't know."

"He can't make us do this, baby," Jaicyn said. "What is he going to do if we don't do what he wants?"

Rayshawn didn't know what to say. King had earned his reputation in Washington Heights for a reason. People just didn't cross him or not do what he said, not if they wanted to keep breathing.

"I don't want to think about that."

Rayshawn signaled for a waitress and ordered a bottle of Hennessy. He poured himself a shot and threw it down quickly. There had to be a way around King's directive. He just needed time to figure it out.

CHAPTER 15

Jaicyn looked outside the window and felt disgusted. For the first time, since moving to Atlanta, she hated the weather. All of her life she'd lived in Ohio where the winters were brutal and it was common to step outside to four or five feet of snow with the temperature ten degrees below zero. She thought she left all of that behind when she and Rayshawn moved to Atlanta. But on the fifteenth day of January, it was snowing and Jaicyn was pissed.

"Why do you keep looking out of the window?" Rayshawn asked. "That snow isn't going to disappear in five minutes. It's cold as hell out there."

"Isn't that an oxymoron?" Rickie giggled. "Hell isn't cold."

"Shut up," Jaicyn snapped. "Play your game."

The family was gathered in the living room. They'd started to do things together more often since Rayshawn got out of jail two months ago. Rayshawn, Rickie, and Bobbie were playing Monopoly while Jaicyn was looking through bridal magazines. She'd put off planning her wedding long enough.

Autumn was supposed to be in Atlanta helping with the wedding planning, but she had decided to stay in Cincinnati until Dayshawn was ready to give her the type of commitment she wanted.

All Jaicyn wanted was to focus on her wedding but she couldn't. The weather was making her depressed and every time Rayshawn's phone rang, she got nervous. Without Johnny around to handle distribution, Rayshawn was back in the saddle. He was doing exactly what King wanted him to do. Backing out was too dangerous. They couldn't take that risk, not now.

Rayshawn wanted to wait until they girls were out of school for the summer before approaching King again. Johnny told him that Little Man was getting out in the spring. With Little Man free, the south side could pick back up. King wouldn't be so dependent on what Rayshawn was doing in Atlanta. Summer was perfect timing.

"You've been really cranky lately," Rayshawn commented, while the girls groaned when his corvette landed on Free Parking and he collected all of the tax money they'd stashed there.

"I think I'm getting sick," Jaicyn answered. "I haven't been feeling right for a couple of days."

"Go to the doctor," Rayshawn said. "You need a checkup anyway."

"Maybe you're preggers," Bobbie smiled. She and Rickie wouldn't mind having a niece or nephew around. It would be fun.

"I'm not pregnant," Jaicyn countered. "I'm fine. Just overworked. We need to take a vacation."

"I offered to take you on vacation for Christmas," Rayshawn reminded her. "But you wanted to stay here. Now we have to wait until the summer."

"Maybe y'all should go somewhere for the weekend," Rickie suggested, hoping that Rayshawn and Jaicyn would leave for a few days.

She loved them to death but sometimes Jaicyn acted like her mother and sometimes she acted like her sister. Rickie never knew which one she was going to get when she woke up in the morning. She hated when Jaicyn tried to act like their mother. She didn't want to hurt Jaicyn's feelings by pointing out the obvious but they didn't have a mother. Their mother was dead.

"I need more than a weekend," Jaicyn vented.

Rayshawn and the girls ignored Jaicyn's frustrated outburst and focused on their game. Rayshawn was winning but Rickie and Bobbie were determined that he wouldn't. He'd already beat them at Madden and they'd quit before they let him beat them at Monopoly which was a stupid game anyway.

"I don't want to play this anymore. Let's play Rock Band," Bobbie announced.

"Do not turn that game on," Jaicyn warned. "I don't feel like hearing it."

"Then go watch TV in the bedroom," Rayshawn replied. "We're trying to chill and your cranky ass ain't gonna ruin it."

Jaicyn glared at Rayshawn but grabbed her magazine and stormed down the hall to her bedroom.

Rickie, Bobbie, and Rayshawn looked at each other and laughed. Bobbie turned on the PlayStation 3 while Rickie and Rayshawn put up the Monopoly game.

From her bedroom Jaicyn could hear the three of them playing the game and got even more irritated. Jaicyn shut her magazine and turned on the television, trying to drown out the fun her family was having. She knew what was wrong with her. She wasn't sick. She had cabin fever. She wanted a new house in some place warm. She wanted to live the life she had before Rayshawn got locked up. The girls may have learned to be patient in the apartment but Jaicyn's patience was wearing thin.

They couldn't move though. Rayshawn was being more careful than before. He thought the FEDS might still be watching him. Until King gave him the okay to move on, they had to stay in the apartment.

Rayshawn slipped open the bedroom door a few hours later and walked in the room. Even with the lights out, he could still see the semi-permanent scowl etched on his fiancée's face.

He moved the stack of bridal magazines to the floor. "Did you see anything you liked?"

"Yeah, I just have to find a shop here that carries them. Plus I want Autumn, Taylor, and Joy here with me when I go dress shopping."

"Joy and Taylor? I haven't heard those names in months."

"I talk to Joy and Taylor practically every day," Jaicyn argued. "I don't talk about them to you because you don't like them."

"Are they still working in the Park?"

Jaicyn shook her head. "Nope. Sabrina came back with her girlfriend and Little Man put her back to work. You should know that. Don't they keep you in the loop anymore?"

Rayshawn tried to ignore the stinging bit of sarcasm that infiltrated Jaicyn's words, but he was sick of it. He was tired of babying her and letting her get away with having the worst attitude in the world, twenty-four hours a day.

"This shit isn't easy for me either," he replied. "Don't think for a second that you're the only one pissed off at King. What the hell do you want me to do?"

Jaicyn rolled her eyes and turned her back to Rayshawn. "If you had done what I said last year, we would have been gone. We could be living the good life in Puerto Rico instead of waiting for you to get locked up again."

"If you wanted to live in Puerto Rico so fuckin' bad, you should have left Washington Heights with your grandmother when you came back from Job Corps. You made the decision to stay and be a part of this with me. Deal with it. If you have a better plan than running off to Puerto Rico, I'm all ears. If not, shut up about it."

"Shut up?" Jaicyn grumbled with her back still towards Rayshawn. "Is that how you talk to your fiancée?"

"When she's constantly PMSing...yes," Rayshawn replied and turned the station to ESPN. "I don't know what else to say to you, Jay-Jay. I just need you to trust me. Trust that I know what I'm doing. And when I said summer, I meant it."

"How much this time?" she asked, referring to the last delivery one of Cesar's drivers had unloaded into their storage unit earlier that day.

"Five."

Jaicyn sat up quickly like a bolt of electricity had shocked her and turned on the bedside lamp.

"Five!" she yelled. "How is keeping five million dollars worth of dope in a damn storage unit keeping a low profile? How is that helping us? We can't get rid of all of that dope on our own."

"Relax," Rayshawn said coolly. "Most of it is going to a new contact in Charlotte. The rest is going to Miami. We're done in Atlanta."

"Whatever you say, Rayshawn. But you and King are getting greedy. Three last month, five this month. Greed begets stupidity."

"You've never complained about money before," Rayshawn answered. "Don't start now."

"Maybe if you focused on more of what you want to do and less on what King needs from you, then you wouldn't be taking these risks and I wouldn't have a reason to complain."

"Summer!" Rayshawn yelled. "Just wait, damn it! I can't focus on anything else but this until then. Why can't you understand that?"

"Stop hollerin' at me! You do what you have to do and I'll do what I have to do until summer!"

Jaicyn hopped out of the bed, snatched the comforter and walked out of the room. Rayshawn didn't go after her. There was no point. If she didn't understand why he was doing what King wanted, there was no way he could make her.

King was testing him. He was testing Rayshawn's loyalty. He wanted to be sure that Rayshawn wasn't a snitch. Words weren't good enough. Rayshawn had to prove his loyalty again. By asking for permission to walk away, he'd done something he'd never done before; shown fear.

King did not accept or respect fear. After all the years with Rayshawn, teaching him the ropes, King was disappointed and he had to prove, once again, that he could handle himself. His life depended on it.

CHAPTER 16

After deliberately missing two doctor's appointments in two weeks, Jaicyn decided to man up and actually go. The girls in the shop insisted on it. Her eyes were shallow and her energy was down. Toya thought she was anemic.

Over the last two weeks she'd tried everything to put some pep in her step. She drank energy drinks and popped vitamins, still nothing helped. Now she had to seek medical attention. She insisted that Rayshawn come with her because not only didn't she want to hear any bad news alone.

After the nurse took her vitals and she gave a urine and blood sample, Jaicyn and Rayshawn were alone in the examination room, waiting for the doctor to come in. Rayshawn was in a pissy mood and Jaicyn was irritated. He hadn't spoken at all on the ride to the doctor's office.

"Rayshawn, what's wrong with you?" Jaicyn snapped. "Why do you look so pissed?"

"I'm not talking about it here," Rayshawn muttered.

"You might as well talk about it here," Jaicyn replied. "There's no privacy in that little ass apartment."

Rayshawn took a deep agitated breath. She'd been nagging him all morning about what was on his mind. If she asked one more time, he was going to snap.

"Rayshawn!"

"Jay-Jay, will you please be quiet. I'll tell you later."

"Tell me what later?" Jaicyn demanded.

"Fuck it," Rayshawn said aloud. If she wanted to know right then and there then she should know. He sure as hell wasn't going to listen to her nag him for another couple of hours.

"King's locked up," Rayshawn said calmly. "DEA raided King Cars last night. The crew wants us to come to Washington Heights."

"Hell fucking no!" Jaicyn yelled. "You said we were getting out of this shit!"

"I know what I said," Rayshawn stated in a normal voice. Usually when he kept his voice calm and even Jaicyn stopped yelling and used her indoor voice.

"Then tell the crew to kiss your ass," Jaicyn answered. "I'm sure that Blaque and Slim can run that makeshift crew by themselves. They only want you so they can continue to eat."

"Don't act like you didn't know they'd want us home," Rayshawn replied.

"But we don't have to go," Jaicyn said. "We can't. It's too risky. If the FEDS are still watching you, then running back to Washington Heights is only going to make it worse. It's too obvious, Rayshawn."

"Don't you think I know that?"

"Besides," Jaicyn ignored the fact that Rayshawn had just spoken. "The crew isn't the same. They don't care about us anymore. We hardly hear from them at all, except Johnny and Blaque every now and then."

"Yeah, but I'm the only one who knows who the connect is."

"This is our opportunity to let all of this shit go, baby," Jaicyn pleaded but she could see the resistance in Rayshawn's eyes. He still cared about his friends back home even if they didn't give a shit about him.

"We were all cool before. I can't just let them down like that."

Jaicyn stared at the plain tile floor. "Why not? They let you down. They didn't care that you got locked up because I was down here making sure that King still got money to make sure they still worked."

"Cesar's going back to Columbia," Rayshawn said out of the blue. Jaicyn looked up quickly. That only meant one thing. They were done.

"What are you saying?"

Before he could respond Dr. Moreno entered the exam room. She was younger than Jaicyn's last doctor. The best thing was she was Puerto Rican. Jaicyn was thrilled.

"So, Jaicyn, how long have you been feeling bad?" Dr. Moreno asked while she looked at Jaicyn's chart.

Jaicyn was about to lie and say a couple of days but Rayshawn was there and he knew the truth. If she lied he'd just tell the doctor the truth.

"About a month," Jaicyn answered. "I think I might be anemic."

Rayshawn rolled his eyes at his fiancée's diagnosis. She wasn't a doctor. She didn't know what the hell was wrong with her.

"Well," Dr. Moreno commented, "you're definitely anemic. And you are about eleven weeks pregnant.

"What?" Rayshawn sputtered before Jaicyn could even utter a word. "She's pregnant?"

"Shut. Up," Jaicyn said slowly. "You're kidding right?"

Jaicyn was in shock. She hadn't even realized that she missed her period. Three months pregnant? No!

"No, I'm not kidding," Dr. Moreno smiled.

"This is crazy," Jaicyn said, unable to believe that a baby was the culprit behind her sickness.

"I can't believe you didn't know," Rayshawn said to Jaicyn. "How do you miss three periods and not suspect something?"

"If I wasn't so stressed, maybe I would have noticed," Jaicyn defended herself. "Besides, you know my cycle better than me. How come you didn't notice?"

"Because I live in a house full of girls! When one of you is on your period I just figure that you all are. You all act the same."

"Oh my God," Jaicyn said. "I can't believe this. Are you sure?" she asked the doctor.

"I'm sure," Dr. Moreno answered. "Your blood and urine tests both tested positive. I suggest you see your OB/GYN soon."

Jaicyn rubbed her hand over her belly. She didn't feel any different but knowing that Rayshawn's child was growing inside her changed everything.

"Can you give us a minute?" Jaicyn asked the doctor.

"Certainly," Dr. Moreno smiled at the young couple. They were taking the news rather well.

"Can you believe this?" Jaicyn asked Rayshawn. "Can you believe that we're having a baby?"

"I can't believe it took this long to knock you up," Rayshawn answered. "Lord knows we've been careless with the birth control."

"Things happen when the time is right," Jaicyn stated. "Rayshawn," she giggled, "we're having a baby!"

"I hope it's a boy. We need some more testosterone up in that house."

"At least the timing's right," Jaicyn said. "You better tell Blaque and them that we are not coming back to Washington Heights."

****

Even though Rayshawn didn't want to go back to Washington Heights and run King's drug operation, he had to do something. He was the only one who could contact Cesar before he left for Columbia and there was only one person in Washington Heights that could do what Rayshawn did and do it well. Johnny had worked with Jaicyn for months. He could organize the crew. It wouldn't be on the same scale as before but at least the south side wouldn't get taken over by the Ricans or the Haitians.

Johnny agreed to meet Rayshawn in Cincinnati but he had no idea why or why Rayshawn didn't want anyone to know that he was near home.

"What's with all the secrecy?" Johnny asked while they drove to the Valdez estate. "You act like there's a hit out on you or something."

"I just don't want a lot of people in my business."

"We're a crew, Rayshawn. Nobody wants you dead, man. All we really want is for you and Jaicyn to come home. With King getting knocked, shit is bad."

Rayshawn nodded but didn't agree. There was nothing that Johnny could say to get him to come home. Johnny was in charge now. The crew would have to accept it and deal with it.

"I can't come back," Rayshawn told his friend. "That's why we're doing this today."

"So, you're giving everything up for Jaicyn, huh?" Johnny shook his head. "That's weak. She ain't the first hood chick to get pregnant by a hustler. The game doesn't stop because of a kid. We all have kids, man. King is gonna be pissed."

"I don't care," Rayshawn practically yelled. "My family is all that I care about. King turned his back on me a long time ago. I'm out and you're up. That's all they need to worry about."

Jaicyn had been right all along. He just didn't want to accept it. He'd spent a long time living under King's shadow. They were like father and son until Rayshawn got arrested. King was prepared to let Rayshawn take the fall for him and that wasn't something a father should do. It hurt that King wasn't really there for him when he needed him but he understood the game, even if Jaicyn didn't. But if that was part of the game and Rayshawn was sure that he wanted to get out of it, then maybe he would have to be done with King. It wasn't a decision that sat well with him but it was something that he would definitely consider.

Rayshawn pulled the rental car to a stop in front of Cesar's house and cut the engine. He turned to his best friend of ten years and gave it to him straight.

"I don't care who doesn't understand why I'm doing this. All I really give a shit about is that you come out on top. If this is what you want to do with your life, I ain't judgin'. I'm in a position to make sure that you don't end up like the rest of them. But I only got in this for the money. I have enough money. I'm getting married. I'm having a kid. It's time to do something else."

"I feel you, man," Johnny said. "I knew back then, when everyone said King was preppin' you to run the crew, that you didn't want to. You got heart, but these streets ain't for you. They ain't ever been."

"Means to an end," Rayshawn replied and Johnny laughed.

"That's what you always used to say. I respect that, man. You and Jaicyn did what you needed to do. I'm cool with that."

Of course he was. Johnny was from the south side of Washington Heights. He was loyal to the streets that he grew up on. He watched Rayshawn rise through the ranks, patiently waiting for his chance

Now, it was his time to shine. He put in years in the game and Rayshawn couldn't think of a better, more loyal person to keep the south side on its feet. Cesar would start Johnny off small, like he did King in the beginning. Rayshawn would always be there to help his friend and make sure he stayed free.

As long as Johnny followed his advice, he'd be straight. Johnny saw the money that Rayshawn made in the short time that he'd been in Atlanta. If Rayshawn could make money and stay out of jail, he'd rather follow his lead than King's who made millions and was facing life in prison.

CHAPTER 17

From the moment that Jaicyn found out that she was carrying Rayshawn's child, everything changed in her household. She and Rayshawn were officially out of the business and were concentrating on their new life…or what was becoming their new life.

Still unsure if they were being watched, Jaicyn put her dream of building a brand new house on hold and settled for a condo in Sandy Springs and overseeing the wedding and baby preparations.

Rayshawn had given up on building a recording studio and partnered with a guy he met in a club that wanted to start a record label. Jaicyn thought it was ironic that his new business partner just happened to be named Andre. Rayshawn thought nothing of it and was actively scouting new talent for this label, Power Records, along with his brother. Dayshawn was thinking about venturing into entertainment law, and what better place to start than with his brother's first fully legit business?

Jaicyn wasn't involved in the day to day operations of Power Records which was why she was window shopping in downtown Atlanta while the twins met with a local rapper. It was eighty-five degrees and Jaicyn just wanted to them to hurry up so she could get back in her air conditioned car.

Jaicyn fumbled through her purse for her phone while Justin Beiber blared from her purse. Bobbie's idea of a joke, Jaicyn assumed.

"What's up Autumn?" she said into the phone.

"What's up preggo?" Autumn teased.

"Shut up. What do you want?" Jaicyn giggled.

"I got some news."

"Me too," Jaicyn replied. "Rayshawn is about to sign his first act! I told him that he should sign you but since you insist-"

"Jaicyn!" Autumn yelled into the phone. "Focus!"

"I am focused," Jaicyn argued. "I just think you could be a star. Your voice is better than Beyonce's. Come on girl. Just think about it."

"Fine, but at least let me tell you what's going on."

"What's going on then?" Jaicyn asked, hating to put her conversation with Autumn on hold again. The girl's voice was incredible and Jaicyn was determined to make her friend a star.

"King's lawyers gave their closing arguments today," Autumn said.

The Feds had wasted no time in getting a trial date for Andre "King" Carter. They wanted him locked up as soon as possible. The longer he sat in jail, the more time his lawyers had to prepare, pay off witnesses, and everything else that could derail their case. Within a month after his arrest, King was in court.

Rayshawn couldn't decide if he should attend the trial but in the end he decided not to. He'd beaten his drug case. Showing up at King's trial would be insulting and he didn't want to throw salt in that wound. There was no telling what could happen. Besides, he had his own transition to make and it wasn't easy.

The trial had lasted a month. Jaicyn was relieved that it was coming to an end. Rayshawn spent hours online reading the newspapers to find out how the case was progressing. The trial of King Carter was big news in the Midwest. From Ohio to Michigan, all the newspapers were covering it. While Jaicyn wished the best for King, the outcome didn't look good.

King had spent twenty years in the game and there were plenty of people that he had hurt and suffered because of him. They were willing to talk. Murder, drugs, tax evasion, guns, racketeering; the DA charged him with it all and they had witnesses.

"Are they still claiming an unnamed source?" Jaicyn asked Autumn.

There was someone the papers were deeming an 'unnamed source' that had hurt King the most. That person had fed the prosecutor and DEA more information than anyone. Rayshawn couldn't believe that someone in King's crew was snitching and his first thought was that it was Little Man. No one had seen or heard from him since he got out of jail. But then he showed back up in Washington Heights and jumped right back in the thick of things, under Johnny's command so it couldn't have been him. If King went to prison, whoever snitched was a dead man.

"Yup. I don't think he's going to beat this," Autumn said. "Don't forget to tell Rayshawn, Jaicyn. I have to go back to work and he's going to be pissed if he reads this online instead of you telling him."

"Don't you think I know that?" Jaicyn asked grumpily. "I'll tell him. Call me tonight so we can talk about this music thing."

"Fine, Jaicyn," Autumn said and hung up.

Jaicyn turned around and walked back towards the outdoor café where the twins were finishing their meeting. She held out her hand and Rayshawn dropped his car keys into the palm of her hand. She walked to their car thinking about King.

He had a great legal team and lots of money. King had taught Jaicyn and Rayshawn a lot about how to hide their money, but he didn't have the business sense that Jaicyn did. All King ever wanted to do was run the city. That's exactly what he did for twenty years. He ran it like an old school gangster, like Frank Wright or Al Capone. Eventually, just like with them, the game had caught up with him.

"Autumn called," Jaicyn said when Rayshawn got in the car. "She said that closing arguments are today."

"It's about time," Rayshawn said quietly.

"Do you want to go up there?" Jaicyn asked softly, trying to be sensitive to Rayshawn's feelings.

Rayshawn had made a hard decision when he chose to cut King out of their lives but it didn't change the way he felt about the man. Sometimes he was angry and sometimes he just missed him like he missed his real dad. When King turned his back on him, he lost another father and he was having a hard time dealing with it.

"There's no reason for me to go up there," Rayshawn answered. "My presence isn't going to change the jury's decision."

Jaicyn put her hand on Rayshawn's leg and rubbed it while he drove home, quiet and deep in thought. She knew enough not to bother him.

Three hours later, while Jaicyn was napping in their bedroom, Rayshawn's phone vibrated on the coffee table. He looked at the caller ID and was surprised. The area code said Washington Heights and that number hadn't appeared on his phone in months.

"What's up, Blaque?" Rayshawn said into his phone.

"The jury came back," Blaque said gravely. "Guilty on all charges. He got life."

Rayshawn's mouth dropped open but no words came out. He had believed that King would get off

Life! King would never get out. He'd never see his kids or his wife. He was done. He might as well be dead.

"What the fuck!" Rayshawn hollered. "Are you fucking serious? How did this happen?"

"You don't know?" Blaque questioned. "Someone in the crew snitched."

"Who was it? That motherfucker's a dead man!"

Blaque's chuckle was more sinister than funny. "It's one of two people."

Rayshawn didn't like what Blaque's laugh was implying. "And who would that be?"

"You tell me, Rayshawn," Blaque said. "How is it that you were facing some of the same charges six months ago and you're a free man? But somehow, the minute you get out of jail, King gets locked up? Coincidence?"

"If you think I'm a snitch, just come right out and say it," Rayshawn yelled.

"I don't have to say shit. You're a smart guy. You know how people think."

"That's some bullshit and you know it," Rayshawn yelled. "I'm not a snitch! Besides, that's King we're talking about. I'd never do something like that to him."

"Yeah, whatever," was Blaque's reply. "But you might want to stay out of Washington Heights. Come back here and you're gonna have to do a lot of explaining to a lot of niggas who ain't feelin' you right now."

"Including you?" Rayshawn asked. "Because to me, it seems like y'all niggas are looking for a reason to be suspicious and I don't have to explain shit to anyone. I took my case to trial and won fair and square. If you had paid any attention to that, then we wouldn't be having this conversation right now. You can kiss my ass. If I want to come back to that shit hole, then so be it. I ain't scared of none of y'all niggas."

Rayshawn tossed the phone on the floor and crossed his arms angrily. Blaque was showing his own weakness. If he truly thought Rayshawn had given King up, he wouldn't have called to warn Rayshawn to stay out of Washington Heights. He would have shot him without explanation and been back in Washington Heights before the coroner could ID the body.

Rayshawn was the first person they called when King got locked up. The crew depended on him. Blaque was lying. No one thought he snitched. They couldn't.

"What are you down here yelling about?" Jaicyn asked as she waddled slowly into the living room.

She had changed out of her jeans and into a pair of Rayshawn's shorts and a t-shirt. Her round belly led the way into the living room. Rayshawn waited until she was sitting on the couch next to him before speaking.

"They gave King life."

"Oh my God!" Jaicyn screeched. "Are you serious?"

Rayshawn nodded. He looked like he did when he found out King had gotten shot. He'd lost another father to the pen. She couldn't imagine the pain in his heart at that moment.

"Are you okay?" Jaicyn asked softly.

"I'll be alright."

Jaicyn slid closer to him on the sofa and put her arm around him. Rayshawn wrapped both of his arms around her and hugged her tightly.

"If you wanna go see him," Jaicyn said softly, "I don't mind."

Rayshawn shook his head. He didn't want to tell Jaicyn what Blaque had said. Pregnant or not, she'd be ready to kill anyone who threatened Rayshawn.

"No, I'm staying right here. If King wants to see me, he'll call."

****

Rayshawn gave it a week. King didn't call. Rayshawn wanted answers. Bars couldn't keep King from knowing what was happening on the streets. If the crew thought Rayshawn snitched, King would know.

But King didn't call. He sent Blaque to Atlanta instead.

Jaicyn answered the door when she heard the doorbell ring. She was surprised to see him standing on her doorstep and greeted him with a hug and a kiss on the cheek.

"Look at you," Blaque said warmly. "You look so cute, all knocked up."

"Shut up," Jaicyn laughed. "What are you doing here? How come you didn't tell us you were coming?"

"I didn't know. King called me this morning and told me to fly to Atlanta today and see Rayshawn. So here I am."

"Well come in," Jaicyn said opening the door wider. "He's playing PlayStation and you're letting my cool air out."

Jaicyn led Blaque through the house to the living room. "Look who's here!"

Rayshawn looked up and saw Blaque standing next to his pregnant fiancée and dropped the controller. Blaque being in his house meant one thing...

Trouble.

"What's up? What are you doin' here?" Rayshawn asked.

"King sent me."

Rayshawn paused, not expecting that answer. "Why?"

"To talk to you."

"About what?" Rayshawn demanded to know.

"You know."

Jaicyn looked at the two men standing face to face like a Mexican standoff. The tension between the two of them was so thick you could slice it with a butter knife.

"What the hell is going on?" Jaicyn asked. "Why are you two looking at each other like you want to kill each other?"

Rayshawn kept staring at Blaque. "Because he does," Rayshawn said, not averting his eyes. "That's why you're here right?"

"Man Rayshawn, you be on that bullshit," Blaque answered. "Believe me, if I wanted you dead, I'd have shot you already. I said I'm here to talk."

"What the hell is going on?" Jaicyn repeated.

"Jay-Jay, I got this," Rayshawn tried to assure her, but he should have known she wasn't easy to dismiss.

"Don't give me that 'I got this' bullshit. One of you better start talking."

"Will you please sit down before you go into labor?" Rayshawn pleaded.

"Fine," Jaicyn said and plopped down on the couch. Rayshawn grabbed two bottles of Pepsi and a bottle of water for Jaicyn out of the fridge before sitting down too.

No one said anything while Jaicyn looked back and forth from the two people that she respected the most. She was determined to get to the bottom of the situation.

"Somebody better say something," she finally spoke up. "Blaque, why does my man think you want him dead?"

"It's like this, Jay-Jay," Blaque started to explain.

"Don't talk to her. Talk to me," Rayshawn growled. "I'm the one you got the problem with."

"I really don't give a damn who he talks to," Jaicyn stated matter-of-factly. "All I know is that somebody better say something. We've been partners too long for this to be happening."

"This is how it is," Rayshawn said, "Blaque thinks that I snitched on King. Apparently, they all do."

The idea was so ludicrous that Jaicyn burst out laughing. "Are you kidding me? Is that why you're here, for real?" Jaicyn asked Blaque.

"Something like that."

"You're serious?" Jaicyn questioned. "You think he snitched...on King no less? What the hell is wrong with you?"

"That's what I said," Rayshawn stated.

Blaque took a swig of his Pepsi. "Y'all are trippin' because we're talking about Rayshawn. If it was anyone else, you would be thinking the same shit."

"But we're not talking about anybody else," Rayshawn was quick to point out. "We're talking about me. I'm the same nigga who started out on 125th pushin' dime bags with King watching me from across the street. I'm the same nigga who ran Oak Park and was the reason that all those shady ass niggas even had a place to rest their heads at night. And me and you, Blaque, man, the shit we've done together on those fuckin' streets! Now you're sittin' in my house and accuse me of snitching on the man who practically raised me! I can't believe this shit."

"Blaque, why would you of all people, believe that?" Jaicyn asked. "You're free too. When the shit went down, you didn't even get arrested. Ain't nobody asking you to explain that. How come people think that Rayshawn ran his mouth?"

"Because no one in Washington Heights said anything. We all kept our mouths shut. K-ci and Sonny took years for King. But you two aren't there. Plus, you handed over the crew to Johnny. That shit is not sitting well with anyone."

"Who cares what they think?" Jaicyn commented. "They should be happy that they're even working."

Blaque ignored her. "How can you not go back?" he asked Rayshawn. "How do you just turn your back on your crew?"

"Y'all wanted me to run the south side but I never wanted that. I just wanted to make enough money to get the hell out of there," Rayshawn admitted. "I got other shit going on."

"King wants you home," Blaque said. "Point, blank, and period. He said he didn't spend all these years training you for you to back out on him now. He said he doesn't plan on sitting in prison and watch everything he's built come crashing down. That's not the plan, Rayshawn."

The real reason for Blaque's visit became clear. He wasn't there to hurt Rayshawn or Jaicyn. The sole purpose of his visit was to convince Rayshawn to go back to Washington Heights. Jaicyn excused herself. Thankfully, she had to pick up her sisters from cheerleading practice. That was a conversation she didn't want any part of.

"Blaque," Rayshawn said when Jaicyn left. "This ain't right. I have too much going on here. I have a life that me and Jaicyn always wanted. I'm through with the game. Just let me live, man."

"But you knew the plan," Blaque reminded him. "This isn't new to you. You knew that if anything ever happened to King, you were next in command. The plan hasn't changed just because you changed your mind."

"Why can't you do it? You've been doin' this longer than I have."

"Not my plan," Blaque said. "You gotta come home."

Rayshawn shook his head. "No," he said forcefully. "I'm done. I've already handed everything over to Johnny. I spent six months in jail for doing the same shit I was doing up there. I got lucky. I'm not about to put risk everything again to do the same shit that King is locked up for. I may be young but I'm not dumb. I got in the game for the money. Not the power, not the respect, the money. And I have plenty of money so I'm out. King has too many people working for him that want it more than me. Give it to one of them."

"Rayshawn," Blaque warned. "He's not going to want to hear that when I get back to Ohio."

"He can't make do anything ever again," Rayshawn said. "For years, I've been doing what King wanted me to do. I got my girl involved in this bullshit because King thought it was best. I moved to Atlanta because King thought it was time. Fuck that! He can't make me come back to Washington Heights."

Blaque nodded. "No, he can't make you come back. But he can make your life hell. You wanna be watching your back every time you open your front door?"

"Is that a threat?" Rayshawn stared hard at Blaque.

"No, it's not a threat," Blaque replied. "It's the reality of the situation. All King has to do is say the word and your ass is history. Is that what you want for you and Jaicyn?"

Rayshawn was floored. He never thought about King wanting him dead. He never had a reason to. He had to do something. He wasn't going back to Washington Heights and he wasn't selling dope again. He needed to talk to King.

"I need to talk to King," Rayshawn told Blaque. "How do I do that?"

"He can't have visitors until next month," Blaque informed him. "You sure you want to see him?"

"Yeah, but don't tell him nothing. If he wants to know something, he can talk to me."

"That's cool with me," Blaque replied.

Rayshawn looked up from the label of the Pepsi bottle he was playing with and stared at Blaque.

"Are we cool?" he asked. He wanted to be able to sleep comfortably in his bed. He wouldn't let Blaque leave Atlanta if they still had beef.

"Always," Blaque stated. "South side till we die, remember?"

"Cool. I don't want any problems with you. Your ass is crazy," Rayshawn joked.

"I don't know why people say that," Blaque wondered. "I just handle my business. That's all."

"Whatever man."

"So, since everything's peace with us," Blaque stated, "you ain't gon mind if I hang out here for a couple of days, do you? I need a vacation."

"Stay as long as you want. You're family, right."

Blaque grinned. He held out his hand so Rayshawn could give him a pound. "And you know it."

CHAPTER 18

Rickie and Bobbie walked into the house after cheerleading camp expecting to find the house quiet and peaceful. It was after six so Jaicyn would be home from *Caliente* and Rayshawn usually came home late anyway, since he was out trying to get more rappers for his label.

The two young ladies liked having a few moments along so they could chill. They were constantly helping Jaicyn get ready for the baby, plus they had cheerleading practice every day. On the days that they made it home before Jaicyn, they usually had an hour alone and that was cool with them.

Only when they walked into the condo, they walked into a war zone. For a second, Rickie had to look around to see if she and her sister were in the right house. The girls heard Jaicyn and Rayshawn yelling at each other in their bedroom. It didn't sound like their usual 'where's my keys', 'I don't know where the hell your keys are' argument. This one sounded serious and Rickie would have bet money that Jaicyn was crying.

"What the hell is going on up there?" Rickie wondered aloud. She and Bobbie hurried upstairs to Jaicyn's room. Jaicyn was sitting in a chair yelling at Rayshawn. Her hair was disheveled; her face was red and wet with tears.

Rayshawn looked upset too. His face was clouded over with anger and he was throwing clothes into a suitcase. Rickie glanced at the suitcase and then at her sister. Both girls had the same thought. Jaicyn and Rayshawn were breaking up.

"What's going on in here?" Rickie asked, opening the door wider so that she and Bobbie could enter.

"Nothing," Rayshawn said. "Go eat or something."

Rickie ignored Rayshawn and walked over to her sister. She sat on the arm of the chair and rubbed Jaicyn's shoulder.

"What's wrong Jay-Jay? What happened?"

"Nothing happened yet," Jaicyn said tearfully. "Rickie, Bobbie, leave us alone for a minute, please."

Unsure about leaving the room, Rickie and Bobbie walked slowly out of the room.

"You better not hurt her," Rickie warned Rayshawn.

Jaicyn heaved herself up from the chair. Her pregnancy was stressful enough. She certainly didn't need the added stress that Rayshawn was causing her. She shut the door and sat down on the bed, making his pile of clothes fall over. Rayshawn glared at her and picked them back up.

"Rayshawn, you can't go. Why would you want to? This is dumb!"

"Jay-Jay, that's been your argument all day. If you can't come up with something better than 'this is dumb' shut up about it. I'm going!"

"Why the fuck do you have to go to Washington Heights?" Jaicyn yelled.

Just a few hours ago, Autumn had called Jaicyn with some disturbing information. Her brother had overheard some guys in Oak Park talking about Rayshawn. She called Jaicyn right away to tell her what they said.

Jaicyn didn't know if she should cry or just kill Rayshawn after Autumn told her that the word on the street was that people were looking for Rayshawn and if they ever found him he was as good as dead. The most disturbing part was that this order was a directive from King; at least that's what Autumn heard.

Jaicyn decided to ask Rayshawn about it but before she could ask him, she came home to find him packing a suitcase, talking about he was going to visit King. Jaicyn was livid. That's when the argument started an hour and a half ago.

"You are being dumb," Jaicyn continued to scream at Rayshawn. "If niggas wanted to kill me, you can rest assure that I wouldn't voluntarily walk into the firing squad."

"I'm going to Youngstown, not Washington Heights," Rayshawn said. "And you know me. I don't give a fuck what these lame ass niggas want to do to me. Nobody in that damn city is going to take me out."

"I don't understand you, Rayshawn. You're always talking about protecting us. Yet, you've known for a month that there's a hit out on you and you didn't say shit to me. Now you want to go up there and leave us here. What the hell am I supposed to do if someone comes here looking for you? I'm seven months pregnant!" Jaicyn hollered.

"Like I said before, Jay-Jay, get a fuckin' grip. You're takin' this shit to a whole new level of paranoid. No one is coming down here!"

Jaicyn wasn't hearing it. She knew that something had happened or else Rayshawn wouldn't have raced home and started packing, talking about he had to get to Youngstown ASAP. But he wasn't telling her anything.

"Look, I'm trying to get this shit ended and the only way I can do that is by talking to King. I'm only going to be gone a few days. If you don't feel safe in the house without me then go stay in a hotel. You're going to be fine."

"It's not me I'm worried about," Jaicyn fired back. "It's you. Rayshawn, I'm about to have your child. I need you to be alive for that and you acting so reckless is not working for me."

Rayshawn stopped packing, pushed the clothes out of the way and sat down next to Jaicyn. He put his hand on her stomach and felt his child kick.

"Jay-Jay, you're panicking and you have no reason to. I'm going to take care of this. I promise. Nothing's going to happen to you or me."

"I don't see how you can say that," Jaicyn said lowering her voice since didn't want to upset her sisters even more than they probably were. "You're going to Youngstown to ask the man who put a hit out on you to take it back."

Rayshawn wiped Jaicyn's face with his t-shirt. She was upset and her raging hormones weren't helping her emotions, but she didn't know the whole story. She was only getting pieces of it from big mouthed Autumn.

"This isn't coming from King," Rayshawn assured her.

It couldn't be. Rayshawn didn't want to believe that King wanted him dead. That's why he had to go. If the hit was from King then King was the only one who could call it off.

"Jay-Jay, listen to me," Rayshawn decided to be honest with his fiancée. "I don't know what's going on. But today Rock called me and told me that some dude was in College Park asking questions about me. I can't have some stranger running around Atlanta gunning for me. Especially with you and the girls here and the baby coming soon. I have to take care of this now. This isn't anything but a big misunderstanding. It's King we're talking about, Jay-Jay."

Rayshawn's eyes pleaded with Jaicyn to understand. He didn't want to argue about it anymore. He just needed her to let him handle his business without anymore protests or arguing.

"Fine," Jaicyn sighed reluctantly. "Do what you have to do."

"You don't have to worry about shit. Dayshawn is coming to stay with you and so is Blaque."

Rayshawn threw the rest of his clothes into the suitcase and zipped it. Two days, Jay-Jay, that's all. I'll only be gone two days."

"Just be careful," Jaicyn pleaded. "Rayshawn, please be careful."

"I will. You just rest and I'll be back."

Rayshawn heard his brother's car pull into the driveway. "Love you babe," he said.

"I love you too."

Jaicyn watched her man walk out the bedroom and said a silent prayer for him. She had a bad feeling about this trip but no matter what she said, Rayshawn wasn't listening.

****

The next day Rayshawn was sitting in the visiting room at The Ohio State Penitentiary waiting for King. Rayshawn was very surprised to find out that he was even on King's visitor list. Based on what Blaque and Rock had informed him, King didn't look at Rayshawn the same way anymore. Rayshawn was there to rectify that.

Rayshawn stood up when he saw King enter the visiting room. King didn't even look like a prisoner. He had on a pair of black True Religion

170

jeans and a blue shirt. He had a fresh haircut too. He looked like the player that Rayshawn had always known. But no matter what he looked like, Rayshawn couldn't get over the fact that he was visiting King in prison. He felt his eyes start to water when King walked towards him. He quickly put his emotions in check and waited for King to approach the table.

"What's up youngin?" King said when he got to the table. King was actually a little uncomfortable seeing Rayshawn too. He was angry with him, but at the end of the day, there were things that needed to be said and it was time to say them.

When King took a good look at Rayshawn, he didn't see the grown man that Rayshawn had become. He saw the fifteen year old boy that'd he'd taken under his wing and guided him on the streets. King stepped closer to Rayshawn and even though it was against the rules, he reached out and hugged him. Rayshawn hugged him back.

"You alright?" King asked Rayshawn when they sat down. "What brought you up here?"

"No, I'm not alright," Rayshawn stated. "Shit is all fucked up. You should know that."

"How would I know that?" King asked.

Rayshawn glared at King. "Do I look stupid?" he asked through clenched teeth. "Don't try to play me, King. You tell me what's up."

"No boy," King replied. "You're the one with some explaining to do. What's this I hear about you not coming back to Washington Heights?"

"I'm not. So if that's what you heard then you heard right," Rayshawn said. "Why should I?"

King leaned back and folded his arms across his chest. He was used to Rayshawn's defiance. Sitting in the visiting room of a prison hadn't changed anything. It felt like they were in the back office of King Cars and Rayshawn was complaining because King asked him to do something he didn't want to do again.

"You should because that's always been the plan. The city is yours and you got a lot of people waiting on you to come back and get it poppin again."

Rayshawn shrugged his shoulders. "I guess there's going to be a lot of disappointed people in Washington Heights then, because I'm not going back there. I'm done with it all."

King sat back in his chair and stared at Rayshawn. "You're done?"

Rayshawn nodded. "I'm done."

"Why?" King asked.

"Because I don't need it anymore. I didn't want to run Washington Heights," Rayshawn reminded his mentor. "That was your vision and I told you that I wasn't going to do it a long time ago. Why can't you respect that? Why is it a go back or else situation with you?"

"I'm not making you do anything," King replied. "But I question the fact that you can just turn your back on the city that made you? How can you do that?"

"Because, I'm smart," was Rayshawn's reply. "I have a chance to do something different with my life, for me and my fiancée and our kid. Fuck what anybody else thinks I should do. I'm not putting my family at risk anymore."

King nodded his head slowly. He never had the chance to be anything else except a drug dealer. King's came from a family of dealers and that was all he knew. Rayshawn didn't have to have that same fate. He should have wanted more for Rayshawn, especially since Rayshawn wanted more than a life of drugs and guns. King acknowledged the unmoving expression on Rayshawn's face closed his eyes.

"You're right," King finally said. "I can't force you to do something that you don't want to do. You and I don't live the same life. I was your age when I took over Washington Heights because that's what I wanted to do. I didn't give a damn about anything else except owning the city and making money. The money wasn't even that important to me. It's the power."

"But with me," Rayshawn interrupted, "it's only about the money."

"So you've said," King replied. "I respect that you want to be with your family. I'd give anything to see my son and daughter grow up. I'm going to miss that because I never had those kinds of wants like you do."

Rayshawn was stunned by King's sudden turnaround. It didn't change the fact that he was still pissed off. It didn't change the fact that people in Washington Heights thought he was the reason King was in prison.

"If you respect it," Rayshawn started, "then why did you send some nigga to Atlanta to kill me?"

"What the fuck are you talking about?" King questioned.

"You know what I'm talking about," Rayshawn insisted. "You sent Blaque down there to tell me yo come home. I said no and now I'm getting word that niggas are gunnin' for me. Why can't you just let me out of this shit?"

"I don't know what you're talking about!" King said. "No one in Washington Heights should be looking for you. "

King was infuriated. His last standing order before he got sentenced was Rayshawn was not to be touched. The crew was supposed to protect him, not try to kill him! He knew that Rayshawn had never uttered a word about King or anyone else in the organization. Rayshawn was one of the few people that King trusted. King knew who the snitch was. He wanted Blaque and Rayshawn to handle it, like old times.

One last gesture to let everyone in Washington Heights know that even though he was locked up, he could still make shit happen.

"What are you saying?" Rayshawn asked. If it wasn't King, then who the hell wanted him dead?

"You've been set up," King stated gravely. "And I know who's behind it."

"Who?" Rayshawn wanted to know but King gave him a look that indicated it wasn't something that they could speak freely about in a prison.

"Call Slim and tell him to bring his ass home. You, Blaque and Slim find Little Man. He might still be in Philly or he's hiding out at his mama's. I don't have to tell you why."

"I told Jaicyn I'd be back in two days," Rayshawn protested. "I can't go to Philly or Washington Heights."

"If you don't," King warned, "you won't make it back to Atlanta."

The serious tone that King was using instantly clarified the situation. No further explanation was necessary.

Next stop, Philadelphia.

CHAPTER 19

Jaicyn sat up in her bed and clutched her sheet, startled awake by loud shriek. She glanced at her bedside clock. The blue LCD numbers read 9:35. She took her loaded pistol from the nightstand and eased out of the bedroom. When she came upstairs an hour ago, the girls had just started watching a scary movie but that scream wasn't from a movie. Rickie's scream sounded like she was being tortured.

Paranormal Activity was still playing on the living room TV but the only people in there were her sisters. Jaicyn held the gun behind her back and breathed a sigh of relief.

"Why are you screaming like that? Turn the damn station if you're so damn scared! You almost gave me a heart attack," Jaicyn yelled. "I thought someone was down here trying to kill you!"

Rickie reached towards Jaicyn and handed her phone to her.

"Sandy needs to talk to you," Rickie whispered. Jaicyn looked down at the phone then at her sisters. Both were crying.

And Sandy hadn't spoken to Jaicyn in almost a year!

Jaicyn's hands were shaking as she brought the phone to her ear.

"What happened?" she asked.

"It's Rayshawn," Sandy said slowly.

"I know," Jaicyn said. "What happened?"

"He got shot. It doesn't look good. Jaicyn, you need to get here fast." Even Sandy didn't want to go into details over the phone. The situation was too serious to talk about.

The phone slipped from Jaicyn's hand and fell on the carpet with a quiet thud. Her entire body went numb, except her heart. Her heart was pounding in her chest. The harder it beat, the harder her baby kicked.

"Where is Dayshawn?" Jaicyn barely managed to utter to her sisters.

"He and Blaque went to get something to eat," Bobbie answered. Her hands were trembling as she wrapped her arms around her sister's waist. "What happened to Rayshawn?"

"I don't know," Jaicyn wept, "but I have to get home!"

"They'll be back in a minute. Sit down before you fall down," Rickie ordered. "I'll text him."

Jaicyn sat on the sofa and stared at the carpet. The room was spinning in slow motions. It seemed like hours before Dayshawn and Blaque burst through the front door.

"What's going on? Rickie said something happened to my brother."

Jaicyn looked up. Tears streaked her face. "Sandy called. Rayshawn got shot. We need to get to Washington Heights ASAP."

If Dayshawn wasn't so dark his face would have turned white. He looked like someone had just gut punched him. He'd been feeling weird all day. There was a nagging feeling in the pit of his stomach that something awful as going to happen to him or his brother. Apparently, his twin connection with his brother was still intact.

"Is he alive?"

"I don't know," Jaicyn said. "We have to get to Washington Heights now."

"Let's go to the airport now," Blaque said. "I'm sure we can get a flight out tonight."

Within ten minutes, Jaicyn, Rickie, Bobbie, Dayshawn, and Blaque were piled into Rayshawn's Escalade and were off to Atlanta's Hartsfield-Jackson Airport. Jaicyn was disturbingly quiet during the ride. She didn't even say a word as they bought tickets for the next flight out of Atlanta to Cleveland, Ohio. They had an hour wait. Rickie and Bobbie talked quietly to each other, each girl worried about their sister and how she would act if Rayshawn died.

Blaque spent the hour making calls to Washington Heights trying to get information about what happened. The news was coming in fast. Everybody in Washington Heights knew what happened but nobody knew who did it.

Dayshawn was trying to keep from breaking down in front of Jaicyn and her sisters. They were scared and the sight of a grown man crying always scared women more. He forced himself to believe that his brother was going to be alright because if he thought that there was even the slightest chance that Rayshawn would die; Dayshawn wouldn't be able to take it.

Instead, he did something that he hadn't done in years. He called his grandparents. Ike and Yvette had stopped talking to the twins shortly after Jaicyn went to Job Corps. Rayshawn had chosen to completely cut all ties with his father's side of the family. Dayshawn tried to keep in touch but he only talked to his grandparents once in awhile. But one of their grandkids was lying in the hospital and they needed to know about it. Rayshawn needed all the prayers he could get.

Blaque got off the phone and walked back up the corridor to where Jaicyn was sitting and staring out the window. She was in a daze and had been since she hung up the phone with Sandy.

"I just got off the phone with Slim," Blaque said, sitting down next to Jaicyn. "He's flying in from L.A. It looks like the team is gearing up and everyone's going to meet up in Oak Park after we go by the hospital. Corey said that Rayshawn isn't doing so good," Blaque continued to talk even though Jaicyn was ignoring him.

"Don't say anything else," Jaicyn interrupted quietly. "I don't want to hear about anything that's going on up there. I don't want to hear anything about his condition from anyone that doesn't have a medical degree. Just leave me alone and let me think."

Blaque didn't say anything else to her. In fact, no one said anything to her all the way to Cleveland.

During the ride to Washington Heights from the Cleveland airport Jaicyn sat in the front seat of the rented Ford Expedition with her eyes closed. Everyone thought she was sleep but she wasn't. She was thinking.

After she checked on Rayshawn, she had to plan her retaliation. Shooting her fiancé wasn't going unpunished. Everyone in Washington Heights should have known better. Unless King had spread the word, no one there should have known that Rayshawn was out the game. To go after him was the equivalent of going after King and Ramel had paid the price for that.

When King was shot, Rayshawn put aside his emotions to handle the business. Now it was her turn. Only, Jaicyn didn't know how to do that. She didn't even think if she could. This was one time, she'd definitely have to let Blaque and Slim take charge.

It was raining in Washington Heights when the small group finally pulled into the entrance of Park General Hospital. Jaicyn had the door of the Expedition open before Blaque had even pulled to a complete stop. She waited until he had stopped the truck completely before she climbed out.

There were at least ten people standing outside of the Belleview Hospital Emergency Room. All of her old crew was impatiently waiting for her arrival. Moving in sync like the Secret Service, they all rushed over to the Expedition and formed a barrier around her as Corey led the way into the Emergency Room. Under any other circumstances Jaicyn would have found this hilarious, but there wasn't anything funny about this situation.

Despite numerous protests from the Patient Services clerks, which Corey ignored completely, the crowd trekked across the lobby to the ER entrance. Before they could go through the door, an ER nurse stopped them.

"Hold up," she said. "You can't go back there."

"I'm looking for my fiancé," Jaicyn spoke the first words she'd spoken since leaving Atlanta.

"And that would be?" the nurse questioned.

"Rayshawn Moore."

The nurse stared at Jaicyn, a hint of recognition in her eyes. The woman who stood before could not be the same girl who she went to school with!

"Jaicyn?" Leslie Peterson asked. She hadn't seen Jaicyn since she came into her father's deli demanding to know where her mother was. That had to have been over ten years ago.

"Yeah, who are you?" Jaicyn questioned.

"It's me, Leslie Peterson. Do you remember me?"

Jaicyn looked at the nurse. She remembered her. She remembered that Leslie was the one who told her that Angelina was back on crack.

"No," Jaicyn lied. "Where's Rayshawn?"

"He's in surgery," Leslie replied with a hint of an attitude. She knew that Jaicyn was lying. Of course she remembered her. Obviously, ten years hadn't changed her. Jaicyn was still a bitch.

"Are you his nurse?" Jaicyn asked.

"No," Leslie replied.

"Do me a favor then," Jaicyn said rudely. "Get me the doctor or nurse who admitted Rayshawn. That's who I need to be talking to right now, not you."

At first Leslie was going to say no. She was the Head ER nurse and Jaicyn wasn't going to boss her around. But she put her own anger aside and led Jaicyn and the crew back to the waiting area.

"Have a seat. I'll be right back with Dr. Banks."

Jaicyn sat down. Rickie and Bobbie sat beside her. Jaicyn looked at Johnny.

"Where's Little Man? Where's Slim?" she asked. "Where is Marcus?"

"Marcus is on his way," Johnny answered quickly. "Slim's on a plane. He'll be here in a few hours. Little Man isn't answering his phone. His baby mama knows what happened. She'll tell him."

"Good."

Jaicyn looked at the people standing around her. She didn't realize until that moment that she missed each and every one of them. The way they were all gathered around her, offering their support and waiting for instructions, led her to believe that not one of them believed that Rayshawn was a snitch.

In her peripheral Jaicyn saw Leslie walking towards her with the same doctor who'd treated King two years ago. Jaicyn met them halfway along the corridor. She didn't want everyone to know what was going on until she knew first. That didn't stop Dayshawn and Johnny from following as Dr. Banks led her into a secluded section of the lobby, away from the others.

"What's going on with my brother?" Dayshawn asked. "Is he alive?"

"He's been in and out of surgery since he was admitted," Dr. Banks explained. "Rayshawn's condition is critical. Everything at this point is touch and go."

Jaicyn took a deep breath. "What do you mean? Is he going to make it?"

"I can't answer that," Dr. Banks said. "Rayshawn has many serious gunshot wounds. I didn't get to do a full examination before I realized we had to get him into surgery right away."

"What do you know then?" Dayshawn asked. "Where'd he get shot?"

"The surgeon removed bullets from," Dr. Banks looked down at Rayshawn's chart, "his right shoulder, his hip, and his wrist so far."

"Fuck!" Jaicyn yelled.

"It gets worse," Dr. Banks said. He looked back down at the chart. Rayshawn's prognosis only got worse as the list went on.

"He got shot in his lower back," the doctor continued. "He also shattered his kneecap. He's going to need a knee replacement if he survives this," the doctor informed them grimly and snapped the folder shut. "That's all I know. You'll have to speak with his surgeon when he's done."

When Jaicyn looked at the doctor she sensed there was something in the chart that he wasn't telling them. Rayshawn wasn't going to make it and he didn't want to be the one to tell her.

All of a sudden the medicinal smell of the hospital overcame her and her knees got weak. She started to breathe heavily and it felt like the room was spinning. Johnny noticed her swaying slightly from side to side and made her sit down. He left her alone with Dayshawn and went to find her some water.

"Dayshawn," Jaicyn whispered. "He's not going to make it. He's going to die, isn't he?"

Dayshawn inhaled deeply, trying to will away the sense of dread that loomed over the small group. Rayshawn was tough. He was a solider. He couldn't be fighting for his life on an operating table.

This was not happening!

"He's going to make it," Dayshawn answered but fear and uncertainty in his voice betrayed him.

Tears poured from Jaicyn's eyes. As Dayshawn hugged her tightly she let out an anguished wail and put her hand on her stomach, feeling her unborn child kick inside of her. He probably knew that something wasn't right.

After a brief display of emotion, Jaicyn had pulled herself together and walked back over to the remaining members of the Oak Park crew. She sent everyone home, much to the pleasure of the ER nurses. She instructed Sonya to check Rickie and Bobbie into a hotel, but the girls' protests were so obnoxiously loud that Jaicyn let them stay with her.

"We might have needed protection," Dayshawn said to Jaicyn when she rejoined her family in the small waiting room. "Why'd you send everyone home?"

"They don't need to be here."

"Jaicyn," Dayshawn started to say.

"They don't need to be here!" Jaicyn yelled.

Jaicyn fingered her engagement ring nervously. She didn't want the people who looked at her as a leader to see her crumble. Which was exactly what would happen if Rayshawn died. She didn't need Dayshawn's questions either.

For two of the longest hours of her life, Jaicyn waited for a doctor, nurse, hell, even a nurse's aid to come by with some information, but no one did. Not even Leslie who kept peeking at her from the nurse's station. Every thirty minutes Dayshawn mumbled something about no news being good news and Jaicyn wanted to slap him. They were in a hospital! Rayshawn had gotten shot! There was no good news...period!

"Did you call Autumn?" Jaicyn asked Dayshawn. "She should be here."

"She's on her way," Dayshawn answered.

As soon as the words left his mouth, Autumn burst through the lobby entrance, frantically scanning the room for her friend. She saw Jaicyn sitting down and ran over to her.

"How is he? Is he still alive?"

"He's still in surgery," Dayshawn answered.

Autumn looked at Jaicyn. She'd expected to see her friend to be a withering ball of nerves and tears. Autumn had no idea if she'd be able to comfort her. Jaicyn was strangely calm. She looked tired and scared, but she wasn't hysterical.

"Are you okay?" Autumn asked Jaicyn. "Did they give you a sedative?"

"No, but I have to stay calm," Jaicyn rubbed her belly. "I can't go into premature labor and deal with this shit too."

Autumn sat in the chair between Dayshawn and Jaicyn and took both of their hands in hers.

"All we can do is pray. And I know you've probably done it already but let's do it again. Come on Rickie and Bobbie."

Jaicyn snatched her hand away from Autumn's and stepped away from the group.

"I'm tired of praying," she snapped. "Praying has never worked for me." She pointed her eyes and finger to the ceiling and laughed.

"He doesn't hear me," she began to cry. "I used to pray all the time. I prayed that my mother would come home. I prayed that she'd stop using drugs. I prayed that Ramel wouldn't hurt me. I prayed that Rayshawn wouldn't go to jail. Hell, I even prayed that something like this wouldn't happen. So pray all you want, but leave me out of it."

"Jaicyn, don't get blasphemous just because you're scared," Autumn pleaded. "Pray with us."

"Believe me, Autumn, you have a better chance of your prayers being answered if I'm not involved," Jaicyn replied and walked towards the nurse's station.

"Any word?" she asked Leslie who shook her head no.

"He's still on the table," Leslie said. "Jay-Jay, I just want to say-" but Jaicyn had walked away.

She rounded the corner just in time to catch the tail end of Autumn's prayer.

"As a family, Lord Jesus, we come to you in faith that you will hear our voice. We are asking that you touch our brother. We know that your healing virtue is available to those who reach out to You. You have cured the sick, comforted and strengthened those who were sad. Lord, we ask that you guide the hands of Rayshawn's doctors and nurses. Give them healing hands. Deliver Rayshawn from this ordeal. Make him strong, full of life and laughter again."

Autumn glanced up at Jaicyn and continued her prayer. "Lord Jesus, we also pray for our own strength. When doubt or unbelief or weakness fills our mind and hearts, we pray that you will renew our faith and help us focus on Your words, 'do not fear, only believe'. We pray in Your Spirit, Lord Jesus. Amen."

When Autumn finished, Jaicyn wiped her tears on her shirt. She'd never been especially religious, even though her grandmother was a devout Catholic. She believed in God but God had stopped listening to her prayers. She hoped that he was listening to Autumn now.

Jaicyn felt movement behind her and turned around to see Dr. Banks, Leslie, and another doctor had come into the waiting room and were patiently waiting for their prayer to end.

"Jaicyn," Leslie spoke softly, "this is Dr. Massiano. He's Rayshawn's surgeon."

Dr. Massiano pulled up a chair and sat in front of the group who were still holding hands. He looked tired. He'd been in surgery with Rayshawn almost six hours. He had very bad news.

"Hello Jaicyn," Dr. Massiano said. He looked at Dayshawn. "And you must be his brother, I assume?"

"Yes," Dayshawn answered. "Dayshawn Moore. This is Autumn and Jaicyn's sisters, Rickie and Bobbie."

"Are Rayshawn's parents here?"Dr. Banks asked.

"Our parents are dead," Dayshawn answered. "It's just me and him."

Dr. Massiano glanced at Dr. Banks. He wanted him to be quiet. Dr. Banks was not known for his pleasant bedside manor and this situation was too complicated for them not to be sympathetic.

"This is the situation," Dr. Massiano spoke slowly. "Rayshawn is critical but stable. He's in the ICU right now. Did anyone inform you of his injuries?"

"A little," Jaicyn said.

"Well, he came in with ten gunshot wounds."

Jaicyn's mouth dropped open but no sounds came out. Autumn, Rickie, and Bobbie gasped. Ten gunshot wounds! The only person they knew who'd been shot that many times and lived was 50 Cent.

"Are you serious?" Jaicyn whispered.

"Unfortunately I am. Some of them weren't bad. The more severe injuries are what I need to talk to you about," Dr. Massiano said. "And since you and Rayshawn aren't married yet, Jaicyn, Dayshawn is the only one who can make this decision."

"What is it?" Dayshawn asked.

"Rayshawn was shot in the back and the bullet fractured two of his lumbar vertebrae. The way the bullet is lodged in between the bones, even if he has the best surgeon try to remove it, he may never walk again."

"But he'll be alive?" Jaicyn asked. If she had to choose between Rayshawn being alive and in a wheelchair or dead, the choice was obvious.

"Yes, he can survive the surgery. But the likelihood of walking again is about fifty percent after a surgery like this."

"Do the surgery," Dayshawn said. "Call in the best back surgeon in the country if you have to, but do the surgery."

Dr. Massiano nodded. "That's not it, though," he said. "A bullet hit Rayshawn directly in his chest. It missed his heart by centimeters. Right now, it's constricting an artery. We need to perform another operation to remove the bullet but it's risky. If we don't get the bullet out, Rayshawn will die. But with the trauma that his body has experienced, he might not survive such an intense surgery. Plus we don't have anyone in this state that can do it. We'd have to Life Flight Rayshawn to Baltimore to Johns Hopkins. If that bullet moves while he's in transit, he's not going to make it."

"What's his status right now?" Autumn asked.

"He's unconscious. He's on a respirator and in a body cast. Even if he wakes up he won't be able to move."

Jaicyn's chest started to tighten and Autumn squeezed her hand. Rayshawn was in a no-win situation. She was going to lose him. She fingered the gold ring on her finger the she grabbed before leaving the house and remembered the day he gave it to her ten years ago, in the very same hospital.

"Can we talk about this?" Dayshawn's voice cracked. He could barely make sense of everything that Dr. Massiano had dumped on him.

"Of course" the doctor replied. "Just keep in mind that we have the helicopter prepped and a call in to Johns Hopkins. They're expecting him."

"What do we do?" Dayshawn asked, looking at Jaicyn. He couldn't make the decision alone, no matter what the doctor said. He couldn't fathom saying the words that could bring an end to his brother's life. He put his hands over his eyes and wiped his tears.

"I don't know," Jaicyn cried. "How am I supposed to know?"

Autumn looked back and forth between Jaicyn and Dayshawn, both overcome with grief and emotion. She knew that they were scared but to her the answer seemed simple. They weren't looking at the situation like she was. All they heard the doctor say was that either way Rayshawn was going to die, which wasn't true. He could make it if they performed the surgery.

Yeah, it was risky and the end result could still be the same if they left him here in Washington Heights with a bullet lodged in his heart. He'd be dead.

Autumn allowed Jaicyn and Dayshawn a couple of minutes to shed some tears before she spoke up. She spoke in a soft and comforting tone when she really wanted to yell at them for wasting precious time.

"Hey you two," she said. "We have to decide something and the way I look at it, we let them take Rayshawn to Baltimore. If there's even the slightest chance that he will survive, don't you want to take that chance instead of giving up? Because Dr. Massiano was very clear, if he doesn't have the surgery he will die."

"Don't say that," Jaicyn cried. "He can't die. He can't!" Jaicyn finally broke down. She kept crying harder and harder. Rickie and Bobbie looked shaken but they stood over their sister rubbed her shoulders and hair while she cried.

"Jay-Jay, don't lose it now," Autumn said. "Rayshawn is not going to die. He's going to make it. Just let the doctors do what they need to do."

"I want to see him," Jaicyn said, wiping her eyes. "I need to see him."

"So, we tell them that we want them to do the surgery," Dayshawn said. "Baltimore's like five hours from here. By the time we get there the surgery should be almost over."

"I'm going with him," Jaicyn insisted. No one argued with her.

With their decision final, Dayshawn informed Dr. Massiano what they wanted to do. The doctor agreed with their decision. He would have done the same. Anytime there was a slight chance that his patient might live he felt the risk was worth it.

As he prepped Rayshawn for transport, Dr. Massiano was impressed with his vital stats. Rayshawn's heartbeat was strong enough and his blood pressure was decent. If his vitals stayed the same, there was a greater chance that he would survive the surgery. But on the rainy night in Washington Heights, it was the trip to Baltimore that Dr. Massiano was worried about.

CHAPTER 20

Autumn, Jaicyn, and Dayshawn stood together over Rayshawn's bed. In a few minutes the MEDVAC team would load him on a stretcher and strap him down securely in the back of the helicopter. It was a risky maneuver. Even a slight jarring of could dislodge the bullet in his chest and kill him.

"He looks so small," Jaicyn whispered. Rayshawn didn't even look like himself. He was covered with bandages and gauze. There were more bandages visible than skin. It hurt Jaicyn deep in her heart to see her normally strong and healthy man laid out like his next resting place was a casket.

Because the surgery Rayshawn was having was so extensive and dangerous for him, the Belleview Emergency team had removed the body cast and put him in an easily removable brace. If he made it to Baltimore the surgeons there needed to be able to take him straight from the helipad to the operating room. They wouldn't have time to cut through a body cast.

"He's going to be fine," Dayshawn said.

"I just wish that there was some way he could know that I'm going to be with him," Jaicyn said. "That way he'll know that he's not alone."

"He's not in a coma," Autumn replied. "He can probably hear everything we're saying. Just tell him."

"We have to go," Dr. Massiano announced.

Autumn looked at Dayshawn. They were flying to Baltimore with Rickie and Bobbie. It was time to say goodbye to Rayshawn and Jaicyn. Dayshawn leaned over his brother and whispered, "Be strong, big brother. See you in a few hours."

Autumn leaned forward. "Love you Rayshawn. See you soon."

Four orderlies, two at the top of the stretcher and two at the bottom, slowly wheeled the stretcher out of the room, being careful not to even bump the door frame. The hospital staff had cleared the hallway of patients and items that the rolling stretcher could possibly bump. As the stretcher was rolled past Rickie and Bobbie, they waved and said goodbye to Jaicyn and Rayshawn.

"Let's go," Dayshawn said. "We have to get to the airport."

Hours later Autumn, Dayshawn and the girls met up with Jaicyn in the waiting room at Johns Hopkins Hospital. She was lying on one of the couches in the posh waiting area. It took them forty five minutes to find her in the huge hospital. Little did they know all they had to do was go to the Guest Services Representative and he would have personally led them to the cardiovascular wing. After all, he'd known they were coming and was waiting for them. When Craig got word that there were four lost visitors in the Pediatrics wing, he went and gathered them up.

"Hey you guys," Jaicyn said when she looked up. Her voice was groggy because she'd finally been able to catch a few Z's. She hadn't slept in almost twenty-four hours.

"How's Rayshawn?" Rickie asked first. She was glad to see that her sister was calm and getting some rest but they were there for a reason.

"He made it through the flight," Jaicyn informed them. "He's still in surgery. They called in some heart surgeon from New York. He's supposed to be the best. Dr. Massiano is in there with him too."

Dayshawn felt a sense of relief. His brother might be out of the danger zone. If they could remove the bullet quickly and get him closed back up, the chances of him surviving the surgery were greater than ever.

"How long has he been in surgery?" Dayshawn asked.

Jaicyn looked at her phone. "An hour and forty-five minutes. They should be done soon."

Autumn sat down next to her friend. "How are you holding up? Did you eat anything?"

"I'm not really hungry," Jaicyn answered.

"But you have to eat," Bobbie said. "How come ain't none of these doctors worried about you? You're pregnant. They should be looking after you too."

Jaicyn frowned at her baby sister. "What did you say?"

Realizing her mistake, Bobbie corrected herself, "How come no one is worried about you? There are over two thousand doctors here. One of them should have made you eat something."

"I'm okay, Muffin," Jaicyn answered. "Did y'all eat?"

"Not yet," Rickie answered. "I'm sure there's somewhere we can eat after we find out about Rayshawn."

"Here comes Dr. Mass," Bobbie said.

"It's Massiano," Jaicyn corrected her sister and sat up on the couch.

"Hey," Dr. Massiano greeted the new arrivals. "You made it."

Dr. Massiano's smile was refreshing and gave Rayshawn's family a glimmer of hope.

"Is the surgery over? Is Rayshawn alright?" Jaicyn asked first.

Dr. Massiano nodded. "Yes, he's out of surgery. He's in recovery now. He's a strong man. He's still critical, but the important thing is that he made it. His body is in shock at all the trauma it's experienced in the last twelve hours, but he's a fighter. Give him some time."

"But do you think he's going to make it?" Dayshawn asked. "Is he strong enough to recover from this?"

"All we can do is wait and see," Dr. Massiano said. "Dr. Sanji had to go right into another surgery, but I'm sure he'll want to talk to you."

"Can we see him," Jaicyn asked. She was eager to see for herself that Rayshawn was going to be okay.

"It's going to be awhile before he can have visitors in the room with him. He's just had his chest cut open. But I'm sure you can go up to his room and look in on him. I suggest you guys get some rest, especially you, Jaicyn. You have to take care of that little one."

"Thank you," Bobbie said, happy that someone finally was paying attention to the fact that Jaicyn was having a baby.

"I have to get back to Washington Heights," the doctor said. "But I'll call to check up on you and him."

Jaicyn stood up and hugged the young doctor who took it upon himself to travel to Baltimore with them and participate in the surgery. He was definitely a blessing.

"Thank you so much, for everything," Jaicyn said.

"You're welcome. Take care of yourself. You have my number. Call me if things change, good or bad."

"Thank you doctor." Dayshawn shook the doctor's hand and handed him his business card. "There's my information. If you ever need anything, give me a call."

"A lawyer, huh," Dr. Massiano chuckled, looking at the card. "I'll be sure to keep you in mind." He smiled at the family once again and walked away.

Jaicyn stretched back out on the sofa. "Since we can't see him, you should go get a room and something to eat. There are a bunch of hotels and restaurants less than a mile from here."

"What about you?" Autumn asked. "You need clothes and sleep and food. What are you going to do?"

"I'm going to stay here until they let me see Rayshawn. My sisters are practically exhausted. Please take them to a hotel. If you find a hotel that's close, you can be here in ten minutes if I need you."

Even though no one really wanted to leave, all of them wanted a shower and food after sitting in two airports and two hospitals for the last twelve hours.

"I'll take the girls," Autumn volunteered. "But I'm coming back."

"Okay," Jaicyn said. "Nobody said you couldn't come back."

"I'm going to go with her," Dayshawn said. "Are you sure you're going to be okay."

"Yes," Jaicyn said. "Go. There's nothing you can do for Rayshawn now. And nothing's going to happen in the next hour. I'll be fine."

There was nothing Jaicyn could do either but she wasn't leaving the hospital until she saw her man. She hugged Rickie and Bobbie on their way out and insisted that they get some sleep.

"He'll be alright," Jaicyn said as she squeezed Bobbie's hand as she walked past her. "I promise."

****

"Mrs. Moore," a voice with a strong Indian accent said. Jaicyn felt a hand on her shoulder and opened her eyes. She didn't know how long she'd been asleep or whose hand was touching her.

"Mrs. Moore?" the voice said again. This time Jaicyn opened her eyes all of the way and sat up.

"Yes?" she said to the middle aged Indian man in the white coat and hospital scrubs.

"Mrs. Moore, I'm Dr. Sanji, your husband's surgeon. Can you come with me please?"

The grim expression the doctor's face stopped Jaicyn from correcting him. He didn't look like he had good news for her. She followed the doctor through the ICU doors. She squinted in the bright lights and struggled to keep up with the doctor. Finally he stopped in front of a private hospital room that had a separate seating area. Jaicyn peered into the room. Rayshawn was lying on his back, covered up to the neck with a sheet.

"Oh my God," Jaicyn whispered. "He made it."

"He's not out of the woods yet," Dr. Sanji stated. "But he's fighting. We're keeping a close eye on him."

"How long has he been in here?" Jaicyn asked.

"About two hours. I wanted to keep him in recovery while I performed another operation. I checked his vitals and they were good so I had him moved in here."

"Can I go in?" Jaicyn asked. The doctor nodded.

Jaicyn walked into the room slowly. It was eerily quiet except for the humming and beeping of the monitors and machines. Dr. Sanji slid a chair close to the bed so Jaicyn could sit. Then he left them alone.

Sitting in the chair, Jaicyn looked at her man, so vulnerable and weak, but fighting for his life. She rubbed her fingers over the bandages on his right hand and arm.

"Oh, baby," she whispered as tears slid down her face. "I'm so sorry this happened to you. I'm right here, baby. Just hold on a little longer and you'll be fine. I love you so much."

Rayshawn's eyes fluttered. Jaicyn thought she was seeing things until it happened again.

"Are you trying to open your eyes? Come on, open your eyes, Rayshawn. Show me you're okay."

Slowly Rayshawn's eyes opened. Jaicyn moved to the top of the bed and leaned over.

"Can you talk?" she said softly. "Can you say anything?"

"Hi," Rayshawn mumbled weakly but it was the most beautiful sound Jaicyn had ever heard.

"Hi," she whispered back and the tears started to fall once again.

"Don't….cry," the words came out slowly as Rayshawn struggled through the pain and the medication. "I….love…you."

"I love you too," Jaicyn said. "We all love you. That's why you're going to make it," Jaicyn assured him.

"I…don't-"

"Ssh," Jaicyn hushed him. "You're going to make it. Your son needs you."

Rayshawn's eyes filled with tears. She had kept the sex of the baby a secret from everyone because she wanted to see the look on Rayshawn's face in the delivery room when the doctor announced 'It's a Boy!' But she had to give him a reason to fight against the pain, a reason to live. What better reason than his son?

"A...boy?" Rayshawn whispered slowly.

"Yes, a boy. And he'll be here in a couple of months. Then after that, we're getting married. I know you didn't forget about our wedding," Jaicyn said.

The tears rolled down Rayshawn's face. Jaicyn wiped away every tear with a tissue.

"Don't you cry, Rayshawn," Jaicyn ordered. "I'll do that."

"Jay....Jay," Rayshawn spoke. Jaicyn closed her eyes. It felt so good to hear him say her name. "Remember....your...promise...ring?"

Jaicyn fingered the gold band that she wore on her ring finger along with her engagement ring.

"Of course, baby."

"Want... married....now?" It was a tough sentence for Rayshawn to get out but he managed it. He was in so much pain he couldn't even form sentences.

"Do I want to get married now?" Jaicyn asked. Rayshawn nodded his head once. Jaicyn couldn't believe it. But before she could answer Dayshawn, Autumn, and Rickie and Bobbie were led into the private seating area by Rayshawn's nurse.

Dayshawn came into the room first. He saw Rayshawn's eyes half opened and smiled. He walked over to the bed and leaned over.

"What's up soldier?" he said to his brother.

A slight smile appeared on Rayshawn's face.

"He can't talk much," Jaicyn forewarned. "And he's getting tired."

"How long has he been awake?" Autumn asked.

"Just a few minutes," Jaicyn replied. "I'll give you some time with him before he drifts back to sleep."

Jaicyn made a beeline for the door, pondering what Rayshawn had just asked her. She was positive that she'd heard him correctly. But why now? Especially when she had been planning an extravagant wedding for months?

Jaicyn found a vending machine and put in a dollar for a bottle of water. Along with some cheese crackers and a can of warm ginger ale that a nurse forced her to eat earlier, it was all she had put in her mouth in a day. When she went back to Rayshawn's room, Autumn, Dayshawn and the girls were sitting in the separate seating area watching T.V. Jaicyn peeked into Rayshawn's room. He was sleeping again.

"You guys," Jaicyn said in a low tone. "I have to tell you something."

"What?" Autumn said.

"When I was in there with him, right before you guys came in, Rayshawn asked me if I wanted to get married now." Jaicyn looked at the faces of her best friends.

"Why?" Dayshawn asked. "Why would he want to do that when your wedding is four months away?"

"I don't know," Jaicyn moaned. "He just said it.

"Maybe he wants to marry you now because he doesn't know if he's going to make it," Rickie suggested. "Maybe he just wants to keep his promise."

"Oh my God, Jaicyn," Bobbie said excitedly, "you have to do it. This is just like a Nicholas Sparks book. You have to marry him, today, right now."

"That's stupid," Dayshawn said. "He's in and out of consciousness, so doped up that he can barely stay awake for more than two minutes. He doesn't really want to get married right now."

"I'm going to do it," Jaicyn stated. "I'm going to find the chaplain and I'm going to marry him."

"We'll do it," Bobbie volunteered. "Rickie and I will find the chaplain. You go wash your face. You can't look like crap on your wedding day."

Rickie and Bobbie hopped off the sofa and walked off in search of a Guest Services Rep to lead them to a chaplain.

"Are you sure about this?" Autumn asked Jaicyn after Dayshawn had gotten up to go check on his brother, mumbling something about foolish girls as he walked away.

"This may sound like a crazy thing to do, but I'm doing it, Autumn. It's what Rayshawn wants. I don't know why he wants it. Maybe my sisters are right," Jaicyn shuddered. "Maybe he doesn't think he's going to make it. Lord knows no one else but us believes that he is. And as much as I don't want to think about it, what if he doesn't get better?"

Jaicyn started crying really hard and Autumn put her arm around Jaicyn's shoulders.

"Jay-Jay, if Rayshawn doesn't think that he's going to make it, then you have to be the strong one. If you marry him now or four months from now, it doesn't matter to me. Do whatever you have to do to get through this ordeal."

All of a sudden a loud beeping sound pierced the air. Jaicyn looked towards Rayshawn's room where Dayshawn stood, looking terrified. The beeping and buzzing sound was coming from inside the room. Two nurses and two doctors came racing into the room and pushed Dayshawn out.

Jaicyn and Autumn hurried to the doorway and watched as the nurses worked frantically to adjust monitors and take Rayshawn's pulse.

"His blood pressure's dropping fast," one of the nurses yelled.

"He has a clot!" a doctor yelled. "Get me twenty MGs of heparin now!"

The heart monitor slowed to an alarming rate. Jaicyn grabbed Dayshawn's hand. Her eyes darted frantically around.

"Come on people," the doctor yelled. "We're losing him!"

"No," Jaicyn screamed. "Nooo!" She tried to enter the room but couldn't get past the nurses, all the while screaming Rayshawn's name.

"Get her out of here," the doctor yelled.

Dayshawn grabbed Jaicyn's arm and pulled her out of the room. A nurse raced past her with a needle. She pushed the needle into Rayshawn's chest and pushed the plunger. Within seconds, the heart monitor started to beep faster.

"He's okay," the nurse said. "His blood pressure is rising."

The sweaty faced doctor wiped his face with a tissue. "Good job, people. Let's just hope that's it."

The nurses and doctor walked out of the room.

"What the hell was that?" Jaicyn yelled at them. "I thought he was fine!"

"Young lady, that boy is far from fine," the resident doctor said sharply. "We're hoping he makes it through the next twenty-four hours. If he does, it will be a miracle."

The doctor walked away, still wiping beads of sweat from his head. He hated situations like this. The boy lying in that bed couldn't have been older than twenty-five and it was obvious he was about to be a father. But the chances of him ever seeing his kid were slim to none. Dr. Sanji had done everything that he could but the bottom line was that Rayshawn's body was weak and traumatized. He couldn't withstand an invasive surgery like the one Dr. Sanji had performed. The doctor looked up and saw one of chaplains walking towards the boy's family.

Good, he thought, *they're going to need him. Only God can bring that boy through this.*

"What happened?" Rickie asked, alarmed by the distraught expression on her sister's face.

"We almost lost him," Dayshawn answered, his voice barely above a whisper. "We almost lost him."

"Son, the chaplain said, "do you want me to pray with you."

"No," Jaicyn replied. "Can you perform a marriage ceremony?"

Dayshawn shot an angry glare at Jaicyn. She couldn't be serious. His brother almost died, for the third time that night and she was still talking about that stupid marriage bullshit.

The chaplain wasn't surprised. In fact, deathbed weddings were common. There was nothing worse to a mother-to-be than to lose the man she loved and have the baby out of wedlock.

"If he's conscious," he answered. "If he's conscious and can talk, I can perform a quick ceremony but it won't be legal. If that's what you want, I'll be happy to do it."

Jaicyn nodded. "It's what we want."

There was no way she wasn't doing it now. That episode had scared the hell out of her. If he didn't survive the next twenty-four hours, at least he would go with the comfort of knowing that he'd done everything that he promised her. And he never promised her that he'd be around forever.

After a brief visit to the restroom to compose herself, Jaicyn, Dayshawn, Autumn, Rickie, Bobbie, and the chaplain gathered around

Rayshawn's bed. Autumn had spent the ten minutes Jaicyn was in the bathroom trying to get Rayshawn to wake up while his brother sulked in a chair. Rayshawn looked as alert as he could and Jaicyn stood by his side, holding his hand that wasn't bandaged.

"Dearly beloved," the chaplain started. Autumn and the girls hit record on their cell phones.

"We are gathered together here in the sign of God to join together this man and this woman in holy matrimony."

Dayshawn glared at the pastor. He was tempted to stop the ridiculousness. The marriage wasn't even real! Jaicyn had lost her damn mind!

The chaplain continued. "This occasion marks the celebration of love and commitment with which this man and this woman begin their life together. I only know what these girls told me about Rayshawn and Jaicyn, but from what I can see, this relationship stands for love, loyalty, honesty and trust. Knowing this, it is my opinion that they are ready to take this most important step in their relationship."

"Do you Rayshawn take Jaicyn to be your wife? To live together in the holy estate of matrimony? To love her, comfort her, honor and keep her, in sickness and in health, for richer, for poorer, for better, for worse, in sadness and in joy, to cherish and continually bestow upon her your heart's deepest devotion, forsaking all others, keep yourself only unto her as long as you both shall live?"

"I… do," Rayshawn said in the loudest voice he could manage.

The chaplain repeated the vows to Jaicyn.

Jaicyn had tears running down her face when she nodded and said, "I do."

"Rayshawn and Jaicyn have pledged their faith and declared their unity before their friends and family and so, by the power vested in me by Almighty God, I now pronounce you man and wife."

Jaicyn leaned over and planted a soft kiss on Rayshawn's lips. At the feel of his new bride's lips against his, Rayshawn closed his eyes. He may have been severely injured and struggling to hold on but he could think, see, and feel.

For that moment, he didn't feel any pain. He didn't feel tired. He didn't feel anything but a sense of peace. Jaicyn was his wife. He'd done everything he could to get to this very moment, the moment he could officially claim her to be Mrs. Rayshawn Moore and the mother of his child. Although he couldn't will his muscles to show it, Rayshawn was smiling inside.

"Let's give the newlyweds a minute alone," Autumn said. She hugged her friend. "Congratulations Mrs. Moore."

When the chaplain and their family left the room and Rayshawn and Jaicyn were alone for the first time, as husband and wife, Jaicyn sat down next to the bed.

"I know why you wanted to do this," Jaicyn said softly. She hoped Rayshawn was still awake and listening even though his eyes were closed.

"But you can't give up now. We're married and we still have long lives to lead. You kept your promise but you're stronger than you realize. I know you're hurting, but you have so much to live for."

"I...can't," Rayshawn whispered.

"Don't keep saying that," Jaicyn wept. "Don't ever say you can't. You're the one who use to tell me that we can do and be anything that we want as long as we have each other. Well, I'm here, Rayshawn. You have me."

The heart monitor blared again and again the team of nurses and doctors bum rushed the room.

"Rayshawn," Jaicyn cried. "Please baby, hold on."

Jaicyn couldn't hear Rayshawn's voice as she was being pushed out of the room by the nurses but she could see his lips moving as he mouthed 'I Love You' before Jaicyn was completely out of the room and the nurse slammed the door.

Jaicyn watched in horror again, as the same procedure was repeated. The nurse pushed the needle into Rayshawn's chest but this time nothing happened. Jaicyn's eyes stayed focused on the heart monitor. The up and down lines were becoming less frequent. Jaicyn felt queasy as the lines became flatter and flatter. The room started to spin and she was on the ground and had fainted before she could hear the doctor announce sullenly...

"He's gone."

CHAPTER 21

Jaicyn eased her eyes open and gripped the sides of the hospital bed she was lying on. A horrified scream caught in her throat and she grabbed her stomach.

Her baby!

Rayshawn!

"Shh, shh, Jaicyn," Autumn put her hands on Jaicyn's shoulders and eased her back against the pillow. "It's okay."

"My baby?"

"The baby is fine," Autumn assured her. "Just relax."

"Why am I here?"

"You fainted. They gave you a sedative."

Jaicyn looked around the dim room. The sun was just beginning to rise over Baltimore. She took a deep breath. Her son kicked a painful kick right in the ribs that brought a smile and sense of relief. Her son was fine.

Rayshawn wasn't.

Jaicyn's breath caught in her lungs. Autumn was in the chair next to the bed. Rickie and Bobbie were sitting on the second bed in the room, watching television half asleep. Dayshawn was the only one missing.

That only meant one thing. Rayshawn was really gone. Jaicyn started to cry.

"What? What is it?" Autumn fretted over her friend.

"Rayshawn," Jaicyn wept. "Oh God! He's…he's gone!"

"No, he's not," Autumn told her. "He's still alive…sort of."

"Sort of? What the fuck does that mean?"

Jaicyn sat up and snatched the IV out of her hand and set off one of the machines. The beeping made her sisters wake up.

"What are you doing?" Rickie asked. "You look insane, snatching needles out of your arm. Lay back down."

"Where is Rayshawn? And what the fuck does sort of alive mean?" She glared at Autumn. "Don't lie to me."

"He's…" Autumn tried to think of the easiest way to tell Jaicyn what happened. "He's on life support."

"He's on what?" Jaicyn yelled. "Where is he? I want to see him!"

"Jay-Jay, calm down. He's in ICU still. You can see him. Dayshawn's in there."

Jaicyn looked like a mad woman as she walked as fast as she could down the hospital corridor. She walked into the room that had R. Moore on white strip on the door.

Dayshawn was sitting beside his brother's bed. The respirator breathing for Rayshawn was the only sound in the room. Dayshawn didn't look good. His eyes were bloodshot red and his shoulders heaved as he cried silent tearless cries. He didn't even look up when Jaicyn walked into the room. She sat in the other chair opposite Dayshawn and stroked Rayshawn's cast.

The pair sat in silence for a long time, listening to the respirator and staring at Rayshawn's broken and motionless body.

"They say he probably won't wake up." Dayshawn's voice was so low that even in the quiet room, Jaicyn couldn't hear him.

"What did you say?"

Dayshawn lifted his eyes and gazed at Jaicyn. His stomach twisted and turned. He didn't want to repeat the words but he had to. She was the woman that Rayshawn would have died for. He loved her more than he loved anything else. As much as it hurt her, Jaicyn had to know the same information that Dayshawn had spent the last four hours coming to terms with.

Rayshawn was gone. He wasn't coming back. The sooner they all dealt with it, the better.

"The doctors don't believe he'll ever wake up," Dayshawn answered. "They want to take him off the respirator."

Jaicyn blinked rapidly and tried to control her breathing. She couldn't pass out...not again.

"That's not happening," she stated.

She continued to stroke Rayshawn's hand and gripped the sheet on the corner of the bed with her other hand. The damn doctors didn't know what they were talking about. Rayshawn had survived surgery in Washington Heights, the helicopter ride and the second surgery, despite the doctors thinking he wouldn't.

"We're not pulling the plug," Jaicyn whispered as her lingered over her man. "That's not an option."

"You can't make that decision."

"What do you mean? I'm his wife. I'm the only one who can make that decision."

Dayshawn shook his head. "You're not his wife, Jay-Jay. That little ceremony shit wasn't legal. You heard the reverend say that. I'm next of kin. I have to make the decision."

"You've already decided, haven't you?" Jaicyn whispered, still staring at her man. She couldn't bear to look at his brother.

A single tear rolled down Dayshawn's cheek. "He's not coming back from this," Dayshawn moaned. "What kind of life is this? Machines breathing for him, never waking up to see his child or his family? Come on Jay-Jay, you know my brother wouldn't want to live like that. That's not living!"

Jaicyn's shoulders hunched and she leaned forward to rest her head on Rayshawn's bed. Dayshawn was telling the truth, but she couldn't let him go. She wasn't ready.

"He's your brother, Dayshawn. You can't do this to him."

"I didn't do this to him," Dayshawn yelled angrily. "I didn't kill my brother!"

"He's not dead!" Jaicyn cried.

She hadn't heard what the doctors had told Dayshawn. She hadn't spent the last four hours hearing the words "won't wake up" swirling around in his head, like a scratched CD. In every sense of the word, Rayshawn was dead. Only the respirator and the machines were keeping him alive. Someone had killed his brother in Washington Heights and no one was doing anything about it.

"I'm going back to Washington Heights," Dayshawn told Jaicyn. "You can sit here and cry, but I'm going to find out who did this to my brother and take care of it."

Jaicyn looked up and laughed. He was going home to do what? Dayshawn had never gotten his hands dirty doing anything. He didn't know what the hell he was talking about.

"You're going to take care of it?" she said skeptically. "You?"

"Yes."

Jaicyn laughed again. "You're going to get yourself killed. I will handle this. Don't you know me at all? No one is scared of you, Dayshawn, but those niggas back home know me. They know I'm not going to let this shit go unhandled. They will feel my wrath. You just be cool. As soon as Rayshawn wakes up, I'll take care of this. So stop with all the going home and pulling the plug shit you're talking. Maybe you should go back to the hotel and get some sleep."

Dayshawn watched as Jaicyn went back to stroking Rayshawn's hand and staring at him. He'd let her have her moment because she still hadn't talked to the doctors. He didn't want her too stressed because she was still carrying his brother's child. Once she heard Dr. Sanji's opinion on the situation, she'd understand that they didn't have a choice but turn the machines off.

But no matter what she said, she couldn't keep him out of Washington Heights. At seven months pregnant, she couldn't do anything to anyone, but he could. He needed to right the wrong that had been done to his brother. Rayshawn wasn't the type of person who caused trouble and hurt people just for the sake of hurting people. He didn't deserve to have his life snatched away from him before it really began.

"I'll be back," Dayshawn said and started to walk out of the hospital room.

"Take my sisters with you!" Jaicyn called after him.

Dayshawn kept walking with no intention of doing what she asked. He was on his way home. There were some people he needed to talk to. Plus, he had to see a man about a gun.

****

"Miss Jones?" Rayshawn's surgeon walked past his room and stopped when he saw Jaicyn sitting on the chair next to the bed.

Dr. Sanji had been away from the hospital for almost a week. He hadn't expected to come back and find Rayshawn still on life support and his family still waiting it out.

"Oh hey, Dr. Sanji," Jaicyn smiled wearily at the doctor.

"What are you doing?" he asked.

"We're just watching TV," she answered.

Dr. Sanji's brow wrinkled as he walked into the room. He was familiar with the kind of situation that Jaicyn was in. She didn't want to accept the fact that the man she loved wasn't going to wake up. He saw it often with mothers and wives. That's why he explained the dire situation to Dayshawn.

"Miss Jones, we need to talk about this."

Jaicyn shook her head. "No, we don't. I've heard everything from every doctor on this floor…every day for the last week. And I don't care. I'm not giving up on him. He will wake up."

Dr. Sanji shrugged. He'd give her a couple more days. Jaicyn rolled her eyes at the doctor's back as he walked out of the room. No one was pulling any fucking plugs…not on Rayshawn.

Jaicyn's phone vibrated on the table. She answered it.

"Has Dayshawn called you?" she asked Autumn.

"No. He hasn't talked to anyone at his firm either. No one knows where he is," Autumn answered.

"Fuck me!" Jaicyn grunted into the phone. "What the fuck is he doing? I have all my people back home looking for him. I swear, Autumn, if he got himself killed..." her voice trailed off. The idea of losing both brothers was unbearable.

"I'm sure he's okay," Autumn said. "He's not stupid. He's just dealing with this the best way he can. To him, Rayshawn is dead. He lost his twin brother, Jay-Jay. Rayshawn was the only family he had left. Give him some time."

"What about me? When did I stop being family?" Jaicyn sighed. "Will you just let me know if he shows up in Atlanta?"

"Are you sure you want to do this? The girls want to stay with you."

"Yes, I'm sure. I don't care what Rickie and Bobbie want. They're getting on that plane and going back to school. Who knows how long I'm going to be here."

"Well, I'll stay with them as long as necessary," Autumn said. "You just take care of yourself. And don't do anything stupid, like go to Washington Heights looking for Dayshawn."

"I'm not leaving this hospital. Call me when the plane lands."

Jaicyn sat the phone back on the table and looked at Rayshawn. "You're brother is going to drive me nuts. At least the girls are going to be alright."

She pulled a book out of her purse and leaned back in her chair. Her sisters were in Autumn's care, whether they liked it or not. Her doctor's visit had gone fine that morning, and Blaque was driving in from Ohio so they could discuss their next plan of action. Only one thing was wrong.

Where the hell was Dayshawn?

CHAPTER 22

"Rayshawn," Jaicyn said, "our wedding is still on, you know. You only have four months to keep up this charade."

"Wake up!" She pounded her fists on the thin mattress in frustration. Rayshawn didn't stir. A few minutes ago she thought she saw his eyelids flutter and hours ago she saw his finger twitch. That kind of thing only happened if the coma patient was about to wake up. But nothing had happened.

"I heard he wasn't going to do that," said a voice from behind her. Jaicyn spun around and Blaque groaned.

"You look terrible," he said bluntly.

Jaicyn ran her fingers through her hair. She needed a wash and style badly. She wanted her clothes but sitting around in designer clothes didn't make sense. She was alternating between her jeans and some scrubs a nurse had given her. She couldn't do anything about the dark circles under her eyes.

"Glad you finally showed up," was Jaicyn's sarcastic reply. "You were supposed to be here yesterday."

Blaque stood over Rayshawn's bed and stared down at his friend. "Had a stop to make," he simply answered. "Sit down. We need to talk."

"Duh. I called you, remember? You sit down."

Blaque's dark eyes turned even darker. "Don't give me any of that 'I'm the boss' attitude. That shit doesn't work with me. You need to listen to somebody else other than yourself right now. Sit down."

Jaicyn didn't like being bossed around by anyone but Blaque was serious so she sat.

"Dayshawn's still missing," she told him before he said something that she didn't want to hear.

"Twin is not missing. He's on his way back to Atlanta."

Jaicyn's mouth dropped open in surprise. "What?"

"He went to see King then he came to Washington Heights. We talked. He told his grandparents what happened and what you're doing. He doesn't want this-" he pointed to Rayshawn's respirator, "for his brother."

"He's going to wake up!"

"Don't kid yourself, Jay-Jay. As hard as I know this is for you, you have to start listening to the professionals," Blaque told her. "We knew he wasn't going to make it. They tried, Jaicyn, but it didn't work."

Jaicyn's eyes started to water but she tried not to cry in front of Blaque until he wrapped his arm around her shoulder and urged her to let it out.

"You have to let this go, baby-girl. You, Dayshawn, and his family need to start healing. You need to mourn. That can't happen like this."

"I'm fine," Jaicyn wiped her eyes. "You don't need to worry about me. I know what I'm doing."

"This time you don't," Blaque said. "This time, it isn't just about you. Rayshawn has family, Jaicyn, and they don't want this."

"What you're asking me to do is kill him." Jaicyn shook her head. "I won't do that."

"You're not killing him. Little Man killed Rayshawn outside of his baby mama's house a week ago. This isn't Rayshawn."

Jaicyn looked up at Blaque sharply. "Are you fucking kidding me? Little Man?"

Blaque nodded. It suddenly made sense to Jaicyn. Little Man was in prime position to take over what King left behind if Rayshawn wasn't around. Since he'd always been loyal to King so no one, especially Jaicyn, ever though he would do something like that.

"He was plotting on Johnny too," Blaque added. "King knew. He told Rayshawn that Little Man was the snitch. Rayshawn was going to handle it. Little Man got him first."

"And Little Man is…?" Jaicyn said coldly.

"Floating in the lake," Blaque replied. "I personally saw to it. Me, Corey, Marcus, and Slim."

"Just like old times," Jaicyn said snidely.

"No," Blaque raised his voice. "If it was like old times, then Rayshawn would have been there, but he wasn't. And now you have to let him go. Rayshawn was a solider. He was strong. No one wants their last memory of him to be like this!

"I can't do this, Blaque," Jaicyn wept. "I don't want to see him like this but I can't…I can't let him go."

"At least you get what a lot of women don't get in this game, a chance to say goodbye. You get one last kiss and one last I love you. But don't put yourself or the rest of his family through the pain and false hope that you have any longer. Think about it while I get the doctor."

Blaque left the room feeling a little guilty. But he'd only done what was asked of him, one final favor to Rayshawn and the man he'd worked for practically all of his life. When King called and asked him to speak to Jaicyn, it was because Blaque was the only other person that she'd listen to. He didn't want her to hurt any more than she already was, but King and Dayshawn were right. Rayshawn wouldn't have wanted life support.

Dayshawn was the only person who could sign the papers. He had faxed the documents days ago but waited until Blaque got a chance to convince Jaicyn what was the right thing to do before allowing the doctors to shut down the machines.

Jaicyn listened to the mechanical sounds of the respirator that was breathing for Rayshawn and the steady pump that was continuously draining fluid from around his heart. She ran her hand along the side of his face and cried.

"They're right," she cried softly. "You're a soldier. This isn't living."

Jaicyn rested her head against Rayshawn's chest, listening to the slow beat of his heart. She cried against his chest. Her tears were quickly absorbed into the thick blanket covering Rayshawn.

"I know you tried," she wept. "You did everything you said you were going to do. I wouldn't have made it without you. I love you so much."

Blaque stood in the doorway as the Cardiac nurse and doctor entered the room quietly. The nurse patted Jaicyn on her shoulder but Jaicyn didn't move. She squeezed Rayshawn's hand tighter as the tears poured out of her eyes. She could barely breathe and could not watch the doctor and nurse begin to shut down the machines.

A sharp pain in her heart increased every time another machine shut down and the beeping heart monitor began to slow.

"I love you so much," she whispered. "I will always love you."

The doctor pulled out the final plug and the beeping began to slow until it became just one long flat line.

"I'm so sorry, Rayshawn."

EPILOGUE

"What the hell is taking so long?" Rickie asked, irritated by everything.

"Oh, stop all your complaining," Juanita said. "You know how your sister is. You keep it up and she's going to start yelling. You know how stressed she is."

"Why can't we go to the beach and you can text us when they get here?" Bobbie asked as she struggled to keep her eight month old nephew from dumping his cheerios all over Juanita's new carpet.

"Both of you shut up," Jaicyn snapped. "Autumn just called. They're on the way. So stop complaining. This is huge moment for us."

Jaicyn was anxious to see Dayshawn and Autumn again. She hadn't seen her best friend since she packed up her sisters and moved to Puerto Rico almost a year ago. She hadn't seen Dayshawn since the day he walked out of Rayshawn's hospital room.

The two of them had even missed the birth of her son. Dayshawn was going to flip out when he saw Ray-Jay. His nephew was the spitting image of the twins.

After everything that had happened, Jaicyn wanted to be around people she loved and trusted and Dayshawn wasn't answering her calls. Juanita was thrilled to help her granddaughter make a new start. Jaicyn loved living on the island and the girls were happy living right on the beach.

No drugs...no King, nothing from her old life had followed her to San Juan. All she had to do was focus on being a mother, a better mother than her own had been. Ray-Jay was eight months old and Jaicyn still hadn't gotten used to it.

Bobbie looked out the window and squealed. "They're here!"

Jaicyn opened the door and watched her friends walk up the stone pathway to Juanita's front porch. Dayshawn looked like a black version of Matthew McConaughey in his cargo shorts, tight white t-shirt, and man sandals. Autumn looked radiant in her yellow sundress and matching sandals.

"Hi," Jaicyn squealed. "I'm so glad you made it."

Autumn and Jaicyn hugged like long lost friends. Ten months wasn't that long but for the two lifelong friends, it was an eternity.

"You look so good girl!" Jaicyn exclaimed. "I love that dress."

Autumn laughed. "And you are the only girl I know who can pull off a tube dress at five months pregnant!"

Jaicyn laughed and rubbed her stomach and laughed. "You know I look cute in anything, pregnant or not."

Jaicyn stepped over to Dayshawn and hugged him tightly. "I've missed you."

"I've missed you too," he said and stepped back. He did once over of her and his eyes stopped at her small protruding belly.

"You're pregnant? By who?" he asked. She hadn't been in Puerto Rico long enough to be serious enough with anyone to be having another kid.

"What you mean, by who?" Rayshawn asked from the doorway. "Your brother, fool."

Dayshawn's mouth dropped open and his eyes practically popped out of his head when his brother walked outside carrying his eight month old son. "What the fuck?"

"I told you he would wake up," Jaicyn said smugly. "No one believed me."

"Why...why...why," Dayshawn stuttered. "Why didn't you tell me?"

"You gave up on me," Rayshawn said. He walked slowly with a slight limp. He needed to have surgery on his knee but he wasn't in a hurry to visit another hospital any time soon.

"When I woke up and you weren't there," Rayshawn explained. "That hurt more than any bullet. I couldn't forgive that shit. That's why she didn't tell you. I told her not to."

"Rayshawn," the other twin started to say, but Rayshawn shook his head.

"You don't have to explain it. I know why you did it. It took a minute to understand but I would have made the same decision. We're cool."

Dayshawn, still stunned, made his feet move and walked towards his brother, the brother that he thought was dead for the last eight months. He grabbed Rayshawn's shirt and pulled him into a tight hug.

"I'm sorry," Dayshawn said. "I am so sorry."

"Don't be. We're all we got," Rayshawn grinned. "Besides, there's going to be a wedding on the beach tomorrow. Thought you should be here for it."

Jaicyn smiled at the twins. It had taken months for Rayshawn to begin to understand why Dayshawn had agreed to remove the life support. No one was expecting his heart to start beating on its own. Dayshawn had made the decision that was best for the family and Rayshawn. Still, Jaicyn had a huge task on her hands when she tried to convince him to talk to his brother.

But she'd gotten it done. She promised herself, Autumn, and her sisters, that before she and Rayshawn walked down the aisle and made their marriage legal, Dayshawn would know that his brother was alive.

And she and Rayshawn always kept their promises.

ACKNOWLEDGEMENTS

"The story of life is quicker then the blink of an eye, the story of love is hello, goodbye."

That is a lyric from *The Story of Life* by Jimi Hendrix.

I chose that particular lyric because it sums up what I write, especially the A Hustler's Promise books. The story of Jaicyn and Rayshawn was special to me and I really enjoyed writing it, because growing up where I'm from, I knew a ton of Rayshawn's but not as many Jaicyn's. I love writing strong female characters and that's what you'll always get from me. I promise.

I'm not good at thank you's because I want to thank EVERYONE! Although I have been practicing my Oscar speech for years. All I know is that I woke up the other day with a heavy heart, thinking about the two people that were really important to me and I lost them; my cousin DJ and my grandmother, Lavonne.

I miss them, but I know that with four published books and being an Amazon Bestseller, they are looking down on me and smiling. I hope they are proud.

None of this would have been possible without the support of my mother and sisters. I often think that I'm my biggest fan but my mother comes a close second every day of the week. It's her belief that I can actually do this that makes me keep pushing forward. My older sister Brandy, I thank for being my voice when I just don't want to talk and only want to write. Thanks for signing on to manage my career. We're going to the top!

This journey is just beginning and so far, it's been the best rockiest time of my life! I wouldn't trade one moment of stress for anything in this world. To my fans, you are truly ROCKSTARS! Thank you so much for accepting me and enjoying my work.

ABOUT THE AUTHOR

Connect with Jackie Chanel online:

Twitter: http://twitter.com/JackieChanel

Twitter Handle: @JackieChanel

Facebook: http://facebook.com/ajch79

Weblog: http://jackie-chanel.com

To join Jackie Chanel's secret Facebook group "The Takeover" just friend her and let her know you want to be a part of The Takeover!

Jackie Chanel is a contemporary romance author and self proclaimed writing ninja. When she's not writing, arguing with her muse (McKenzie) or daydreaming, she can often be found drooling over the latest Chanel shoes or playing around on her tumblr blog with a cup of coffee in hand and a little John Mayer or Jimi Hendrix in the background.

Also from Jackie Chanel:
Untitled
Change of Heart
A Hustler's Promise: Some Promises Won't Be Broken

Coming Soon:
Unsung
Caprice
Back In One Piece
Friends, Lovers, or Nothing (A Broke in the City Novel)

Made in the USA
Lexington, KY
08 September 2012